# REFLECTIONS IN THE MIST

Curtis Krusie

Copyright © 2017 Curtis Krusie
All rights reserved.

ISBN: 1544699239
ISBN 13: 9781544699233
Library of Congress Control Number: 2017904137
CreateSpace Independent Publishing Platform
North Charleston, South Carolina

Special thanks to my father, Ron, who inspired a certain character, and to my mother, Cindy, who assisted in copy-editing. Also, thanks to my friend and editor, Paul Tobin, who helped immensely in the development of this story. Most of all, thanks to my wife and cartographer, Bryn, whose unwavering support and encouragement keep me writing.

It had been a journey unlike any they had known before, or ever expected to know. In all this time they had spent with only each other and the endless ocean as company, their love had suffered and fought relentlessly against the odds and their nefarious pursuers, always beating back like the waves against the hull and only a few steps behind at every moment. By the wind and sea their spirits had traveled, and by the same they would depart. As the squall overtook the *Mistical Reflection* and she began to turn over, Grey and Misty spun through the events that had led them to this place, this time, where and when they were both certain they would share their final moments together.

# 1

## Eleven Months Earlier

"October has to be my favorite month," said Grey as he and Misty drove down the Great River Road. Leaves drifted gently across the pavement ahead of the car and wound like snakes in the wake they left behind. She looked at him and smiled, then closed her eyes and rolled down her window, taking in a deep breath of the smooth autumn air. It had been a wet summer, which made for a richly colored fall.

"I'll take it," she replied.

The sound of the great Mississippi flooded in through Misty's window. Above the river an eagle glided, and she thought for a moment that the whole world was on their side. Everything seemed to flow in unison—in one direction. The river. The eagles. The young couple in love.

"The current looks slow," she said. "Almost like it isn't moving at all."

"But it is," replied Grey. "It's always moving."

He watched the cables of the Clark Bridge pass overhead as they crossed from Illinois back into Missouri.

He loved the pattern, the repetition, the symmetry. The bridge had fascinated him ever since it was first opened when he was a child. He had always had an eye for design, a trait inherited from his father, who had served as the principal engineer on the project. Grey, though, had found his calling in architecture.

"Architects make it look pretty," his father would always say, "but engineers make it stand up."

"It's all about perspective," Grey would reply. "The engineer may sustain life, but the architect makes it beautiful."

These same words were exchanged again this Sunday as Grey and Misty visited his father for lunch at his home in Grafton. Despite his teasing, Grey knew his father was proud of the choices he had made, both in his career and in love. Misty was one of a kind, and not lacking her own appreciation for the art of creating a beautiful building. She had been Grey's chosen interior designer on the iconic Star Silo project he had begun two years before that was certain to bring his name to the forefront of the architectural universe before he even reached thirty-five. Over the course of the project their professional relationship had turned romantic, and neither of them could imagine life now without the other.

As they drew near their Kirkwood home, Grey mused over the awkward and eerie turn their conversation had briefly taken, casting a shadow over the otherwise pleasant meal they had enjoyed on the patio.

"What do you think he meant by that?" Grey asked.

"Who?" replied Misty.

"My father, when he said to 'be careful.'"

"Oh, who knows? Probably nothing. He's careful about everything. You know."

"Maybe," said Grey.

Still, he could not move past the ominous warning. Declan was a man of few words who had always trusted his son to make decisions on his own. Any advice he gave to Grey, or anyone else for that matter, usually came through a question that demanded introspection, leading his son to find his way by his own conscience and wisdom. Grey could not remember a time—before today—when his father had told him to "be careful."

And what, he wondered, had spawned such a warning? Until that moment it had been a relaxed and amiable conversation as Grey and Misty regaled Declan with their excited descriptions of the Star Silo, watching as an empty lot in downtown St. Louis slowly grew into a towering work of art, descriptions in which only another mind from the field of design could find any interest; and Declan did. His interest, however, had turned to conspicuous concern when he had asked one question.

"What did you say was the name of the developer?"

"Waterford Real Estate Holdings," Grey had replied. "They're based in Chicago, but they're working with a silent partner on this one. Salvatore Mancini."

Declan had set his sandwich down on the plate and looked silently at Grey as he continued.

"He's some venture capitalist or something. Everyone knows his name, but it's kept off the books. It's actually kind of strange; now that construction is underway we're not supposed to talk to the foreman, the engineers, any of the contractors. Not even each other. They're very insistent on that. No one involved in design is allowed on the site while work is going on. I don't think they know about Misty and me, and I don't want to mention it. Everything goes through Waterford's project manager to relay and coordinate information, and he's always saying, 'I'll have to talk to Mr. Mancini.' I've still never seen the guy. It's all very mysterious. I'm flying up to Chicago tomorrow to meet with him for the first time."

"Be careful," Declan had then said with that unusually stern tone.

Misty had shrugged it off immediately, leaving the names Waterford and Mancini to fade away as she went on to tell Declan of the sailboat she and Grey had also been designing for themselves, custom built by a renowned craftsman in Annapolis. When Grey's business was finished in Chicago, he would be flying straight to Maryland to go over the finishing touches.

"It's our second masterpiece," she had laughed. "It's been a busy couple of years. I can't wait to spend more time on the water. Speaking of which, this meal is wonderful."

"I'm glad you like it," Declan replied. "Just caught this morning."

"I love the smell of fresh fish," she said. "It reminds me of places I'd rather be."

Driving to Spirit Airport on Monday, Grey's curiosity had grown. He was both eager and anxious to put a face to this name, and things had only gotten stranger that morning when he answered a call from a 312 number that he did not recognize. On the other end an unknown man with a deep Italian accent informed him that his flight from Lambert to O'Hare that afternoon had been canceled, but a private jet had been chartered to take him into Midway from Spirit of St. Louis, compliments of Mr. Mancini.

"Your plane is ready and waiting, Mr. Cavanaugh. Take your time. There is no hurry."

Grey exited the highway at Long Road, turned west on Edison Avenue, and as he entered the airport property a black Cadillac with heavily tinted windows pulled onto the road in front of him and stopped. The passenger, dressed in a black Armani suit, exited and walked around the back of the car to open the driver's side rear door before approaching Grey's window.

"The driver will take you to your plane, Mr. Cavanaugh," he said. "Don't worry about your car, sir. It will be waiting at the airport when you return."

"I'm flying from Chicago to Baltimore before I come home," Grey replied, confused.

"Yes, sir. Your car will be at Lambert, long term parking."

Grey reluctantly collected his briefcase and overcoat, exited his car, and followed as the unknown man led him to the open rear door of the Cadillac. The door was closed for him, and the driver waited as the man went back for Grey's suitcase and then loaded it into the trunk. Grey was startled by the sound of the trunk lid slamming shut, and the car pulled off.

The driver did not speak a word as they turned from Edison at a private hangar where the iron gate was unlocked and opened by another anonymous man in another Armani suit. Slowly they rolled into the inconspicuous, unmarked building where the sunlight beaming through the open hangar door framed the profile of a glowing Gulfstream jet. When the car stopped, the driver got out and opened Grey's door.

"Your plane, sir," said the driver over the echoing sound of the iron gate closing, then locking again.

A beautiful dark-haired attendant appeared at the cabin door and greeted Grey as he boarded the luxurious aircraft, and no sooner had he taken his seat than she delivered to him a Manhattan on the rocks.

"Can I get you anything else?" she asked.

"No, thank you," he said. "How did you know this was my favorite drink?"

The flight attendant just smiled. Then she disappeared into the rear of the cabin as the plane taxied toward the runway, leaving him entirely alone for the duration of the forty-minute flight.

# 2

## Chicago

When the plane landed at Midway there was a black limousine waiting on the tarmac, and again, as the driver manned his door and loaded his luggage, not a word was spoken. Grey wanted to call Misty, to relate his increasing suspicions about the day's progression, but now more than ever he knew that he could not risk anyone here growing wise to their relationship. Despite the fact that both of them had been repeatedly informed that direct contact between contractors on the Star Silo was strictly forbidden once construction had commenced, he had not considered for more than a fleeting moment that their love might have them both removed from the project, or worse. He feared that perhaps Waterford and Mancini had already made the discovery on their own, which could explain the sudden and unprecedented meeting request by the man himself. But if Mancini intended to terminate his contract, it made no sense to incur the expense of a private jet and the Fairmont Hotel suite he had booked for Grey, not to mention the corporate staff that had been escorting him with every step he took since he had reached the airport in St. Louis. That alone was strange. Even on the plane, ostensibly alone in that massive, opulent cabin, he had felt as though he was being watched.

Grey looked at his watch. It was only three thirty in the afternoon—too early for the dinner meeting he was expecting. He watched street signs as the limousine merged from South Cicero Avenue onto the Stevenson Expressway headed toward downtown. The driver turned left onto Lake Shore Drive, northbound past Soldier Field, and exited onto South Columbus, past Grant Park, left on East Monroe, right on Michigan Avenue. The car pulled over and stopped briskly behind a bus at Millennium Park as passengers boarded and disembarked, and the driver hurriedly got out to open Grey's door.

"Your bags will be waiting in your room, sir," said the driver.

"Is Mr. Mancini here?" asked Grey as he exited.

The driver pointed toward the park where Chicago's skyline reflected in obscurity from Cloud Gate, that remarkable stainless bean that twisted and torqued the scene from every angle, breaking barriers between real and fiction and turning honest men to drunks in an instant. Before Grey could ask any more questions, the driver sped off, leaving him standing on the side of the road amidst the traffic.

He took his phone from his pocket. Now that he was alone it would be safe to call Misty, he thought, but he had no idea what he would tell her. In just over an hour he had been taken from his own car in St. Louis to the heart of downtown Chicago by a series of unidentified men and left there alone without any way of contacting the one he was supposed to meet. Better to wait until something—anything—made sense. Instead, he called the project manager from Waterford, his only contact with the organization, to see if he might be able to shed some light on the situation. The call went straight to voicemail.

Grey shook his head and sauntered across the plaza and up the steps toward Cloud Gate, mixing with the perpetual crowd of tourists gathered to watch the colors of the world change as the sun and the city were held captive together within the same warped crystal ball. He gazed into his own eyes, gazing back but not quite the same. Face to face with himself he saw one man, a man he knew well, but the further he drew away the more unrecognizable he became. With even the slightest change in perspective came the same in his reflection. He wandered into the shadow beneath, and from above his own eyes watched his every movement from every direction.

A group of schoolchildren on a class field trip forced him from his muse and back out into the afternoon sun. A moment later a hand touched his shoulder.

"Come with me, Mr. Cavanaugh," said a voice. "Mr. Mancini awaits."

Grey turned to find another well dressed man standing behind him, equal in demeanor to the others previous, but more casual in appearance. He followed the man eastward through the park's walking trails, and just as they reached Lake Shore Drive a beige Toyota pulled up to the curb.

"Get in," said the man as he stepped into the passenger seat. Grey opened his own door and climbed in the back.

"Do either of you want to tell me what's going on?" he asked, growing frustrated. "Why all the runaround?"

The car jolted forward, southbound.

"It's just precautionary. Don't worry," said the driver. "For your own safety as much as Mr. Mancini's."

Grey noticed the glint of polished nickel on the driver's hip just below his jacket, then the butt of a sawed-off shotgun beneath the passenger seat in front of him.

They turned from Lake Shore onto Roosevelt, and from there Grey lost track of their location. The car sped up and began winding indiscriminately through city blocks. Tires squealed as they tore sharply around corner after corner, sometimes backtracking and passing through the same intersections two or three times. Both the driver and passenger remained silently focused on the road, methodical in their concentration. They knew exactly what they were doing, where they were going, and how they wanted to get there. Grey refrained from speaking any further, though his heart was racing.

Around the University of Illinois the car slowed down again and rolled cautiously into Little Italy. They turned into an alley and stopped at the discreet rear door of an old brick building with no sign where yet another suited man emerged and approached Grey's door to open it for him. Their timing had been so precise, so orchestrated, and without any communication that he saw. It was as if each man down the line knew where to be at each moment like clockwork. Trembling, he exited the car, and it drove off.

The air outside was heavy and saturated with the aroma of Italian food. Before he had time to ask any more questions, the door to the building was opened and the obtrusive sounds of dozens of separate and boisterous conversations spilled out, poisoning the peaceful silence outside. The man who had opened it led him through the first door, then another just inside that swung into a bright kitchen filled with portly, mustached, white-coated chefs, none of whom seemed to take any notice of the two business-dressed men passing through. On the other end of the kitchen, another door revealed a dimly lit red-carpeted staircase trimmed on either side with gold rope leading to a second floor. The voices from below were silenced as the walls seemed to thicken and close in on Grey with each rising step.

At the top of the staircase, an arched doorway opened onto a private balcony room lined on one side with tall arched windows overlooking the street outside, and on the other a thick wall of glass revealing a scene of the restaurant full of people below, but ensuring that the sounds produced within each of the two respective spaces remained where they belonged. In the center of the room was a square table, where sat a large man with a clean-shaven olive complexion and slick black hair that shone in the sunlight breaking through the windows. His lips grew to a wide smile and his teeth glowed white.

"You must be Grey," he said, standing and extending his hand.

"Mr. Mancini?" said Grey, skeptically, with a firm handshake.

"Please, call me Sal. Take a seat. How was your trip?"

Grey searched for an adjective that would avoid offending his client while conveying his distaste for the charade he hoped had reached its conclusion.

"Interesting," he said.

Mancini's smile endured as if to acknowledge his understanding but declined to provide an explanation. Grey heard footsteps in the doorway and looked over his shoulder as two more suited men entered the room, each looking on as they stood on either side of the balcony's only entrance and exit.

"I've ordered us a two thousand eleven Chianti," said Mancini, calling his attention back. "You like Chianti, don't you, Grey?"

"Yes, thank you."

"Good. I hope you don't mind meeting with me directly. I'm impressed with your work."

"Not at all. I would've liked to have met sooner."

"So would I," Mancini replied. "Things have been complicated lately. You know how it is."

"I do."

The waiter arrived with the wine and poured a taste into Grey's glass.

"He'll like it," said Mancini. The waiter smiled and continued to pour, then moved on to fill the glass of Grey's host nearly to the rim. "We'll both have the Sicilian Duck Breast," he went on. Then he looked to Grey. "Trust me."

"Early dinner?" Grey inquired.

"The dinner meeting is for breaking the ice. This way I've got more time to get to know you this evening."

The meal was extraordinarily delicious, and as the light outside dimmed and the wine flowed, Grey began to relax in the company of this man whose peculiar and even unnerving methods seemed so contrary to his personality. He was at least twice Grey's age and sociable as a salesman, but he seemed genuine—trustworthy—even as he put down three top-filled glasses of wine for each one that Grey finished.

By nightfall Grey was sufficiently buzzed, and Mancini was completely inebriated. Any talk of business had somehow escaped their dinner meeting. Instead it had been consumed with laughter and nonsensical fables from the gregarious businessman. He insisted on a change of venue, and Grey helped his drunken client to his feet. He barely noticed the two men at the doorway who had been watching them in silence throughout the afternoon and evening and followed the pair down the stairs and out into the main dining room of the restaurant. As they shuffled clumsily between tables and patrons toward the front door, Grey turned to look up at the balcony from where they had just come. From this side the glass wall was mirrored, yielding no hint of any hidden room beyond the reflection of the grand crystal chandelier that hung over the heads of every unknowing soul below.

A black Mercedes-Benz pulled up to the curb outside, and the two watchers from the room above handled the doors as Grey and Mancini climbed in. The driver of the Mercedes waited as the nameless pair then entered a car across the street, made a U-turn, and pulled up behind them. Without a word from either Grey or Mancini as to their destination, they were off, eastbound in the Chicago night.

Grey watched the buildings grow and lights vivify as they drew deeper into the city. They stopped on a dark block at the back side of a dimly lit skyscraper and stumbled out onto the sidewalk. By this time the combination of the settling wine and the feeling of fast friendship between he and Mancini had compelled Grey to overlook the day's stranger occurrences, and he had grown intrigued by the night's seemingly endless possibilities.

As they passed through the revolving door into the building, Grey's phone began to ring. Without looking he knew it was Misty, surely wondering why he still had not called. He was still just sober enough to know that answering her call in front of Mancini could potentially unleash a wrath even more formidable than hers, and certainly less forgiving. He reached into his pocket and silenced the ringtone resonating from within the glass capsule.

"Go ahead and answer it, Grey," Mancini insisted.

"I'm having too much fun for business."

"How do you know it was a business call?"

"I only get business calls."

"Uh huh," replied Mancini with a smirk.

They entered an elevator, and the nameless pair, following at a distance, headed toward a second as the doors slid shut. Mancini pressed a button and Grey watched as the numbers on the wall grew. Ten. Twenty. Thirty. Forty.

The doors opened again and light and sound spilled into the elevator like the ocean into a ruptured ship's hull, sucking them out into a sea of moving bodies under flashing lights encircled by a hundred and eighty degrees of bright Chicago and a hundred and eighty degrees of Lake Michigan, black as the night sky. Grey felt his chest beating and wondered whether he was feeling the music or his heart. He followed Mancini up a floating staircase to another hidden balcony overlooking the entire scene below. They took their seats at two plush couches opposite each other where a waitress immediately appeared with two flaming shots of absinthe. Mancini smiled and held up his glass.

"To the Star Silo," he said.

"To the Star Silo," Grey concurred, shooting it back.

"There are two types of people: those who embrace absinthe, and those who fear it. Absinthe was illegal in the States for decades because some politician was told it made people hallucinate. It's amazing the nonsense that people will believe while shunning the truth that's right in front of them. I've been drinking absinthe all my life, and I have never seen the green fairy—not in literal terms, anyway. Even now it isn't easy to find a decent bottle this side of the Atlantic. I purchase it by the crate from Paris and Zurich and have it shipped here. I like to drink in the culture of every place I go."

"When in Rome, right?" said Grey.

"We're past Rome, my friend. This," Mancini opened his arms toward the crowd below and surrounding urban vista, "is Chicago."

With that shot, Grey's buzz turned to a drunk. The two of them continued to banter and drink, diluting the liquor with water and sweetening with sugar cubes, and as glasses emptied more appeared in front of them before they were requested. Grey's vision and inhibitions distorted like the image of himself in Cloud Gate, and the night seemed to go on forever. He felt his phone vibrating in his pocket and turned to search for a discreet place to take Misty's undoubtedly frantic call. Looking toward the floating staircase at the back wall, he again saw the two nameless men, still watching over them and always at Grey's back.

"So, tell me, Grey," Mancini called his attention back, "what is the significance of the name Star Silo?"

"I looked at it," Grey replied to the first mention of business all day, "and that's what I saw. The name means whatever you want it to mean; that's the beauty of it. I saw a towering monument that drew the eye to the infinite unknown above, yet contained within itself possibilities equally bright and endless. But as beauty is in the eye of the beholder, so interpretation is in the imagination of the observer."

"Marvelous," said Mancini, gazing off as if to ponder the implications of what Grey had said. Then he again met Grey's eyes and asked, "How's Misty?"

Grey's stomach sank as the man's smile flattened, his expression in one instant morphing from that of a jolly drunk—a friend with the best of intentions—to the sober wickedness of the devil himself. He froze, speechless.

"Was it not made clear to you that direct communication among the design team was to cease once the project broke ground? You're a thorough man, Grey. I would not have recommended you otherwise, so I know you read your contract."

"You recommended me?"

"I specifically asked for you, and I approved your choice of Miss Sommer for interior design because I thought you were a man to be trusted. Apparently I was wrong, and I'm seldom wrong."

"Sal—"

"Stop," Mancini interrupted. "You must know who I am. I can't imagine that you would be stupid enough to conspire against me, so I'll give you the benefit of the doubt and trust that your romantic relationship is just that. Your name will still be on the building, but you and that girl are off the project. Your commission checks are in the mail. Tell me, Grey, was she worth it?"

Grey stared back into Mancini's six blurry eyes in petrified silence, trying to focus soberly on two. He felt the hands of the nameless pair of men lifting him from his seat, and as they began to escort him out, Mancini stopped them. Grey turned back.

"What would your father think?"

# 3

## The Vessel

Grey awoke in the luxurious hotel suite with a splitting headache and no recollection of how he had gotten there, but a thorough memory of what had transpired just before. The morning sun bounced from the lake and through his open window. Next to the dresser were his luggage and briefcase that had been placed in the room for him, along with his keys and a parking tag indicating the location of his car in the Lambert Airport garage back in St. Louis. He rose to turn down the thermostat, then looked at his phone showing nine missed calls from Misty and immediately tapped the button to call her back.

"Where the hell have you been?" she screamed from the other end. Grey could hear in her voice that she was near tears.

"It's not good," he said.

"What? Are you OK? You're in Chicago, right?"

"Yes, I'm in Chicago. Misty, we got fired. Both of us."

"What?"

"They know about us."

"Oh no."

"Oh yes."

"How?"

"I don't know." He paused before going on. "I think they've been watching us."

"What? You're kidding. Why?"

"I don't know. It's strange here. I'll tell you about it when I get home. I've got to get to the airport."

"Grey, wait."

"What?"

"Are you OK?"

"I don't know yet."

"Yes," she said, answering her own question for him, "we'll be fine."

Before leaving the room, Grey noticed a small red smear on the bed sheets, but he was in too much of a hurry to consider it for more than a moment. He assumed that he had simply cut himself at some point during the evening and was still too numb to feel anything. He looked twice around every corner as he carried his bags to the hotel lobby and caught a cab for O'Hare outside. His mind raced through possible explanations for the unfathomably strange events of the day before, and especially their climax, which made everything previous even more inexplicable. Why the expense? Why the armed escorts? Why the spectacle of grandeur and deceitful performance only to hack it all to pieces violently and relentlessly? He would have been furious if he weren't so baffled. His hangover only intensified with every thought, and he vomited in the back seat of the cab for which the angry driver tacked on an additional fifty-dollar cleanup fee to his fare. Grey gladly paid it. He cleaned himself up in the airport restroom before boarding the plane, relieved to be leaving this city and Salvatore Mancini behind.

By the time the plane touched down in Baltimore Grey was feeling much better, and he rented a car at BWI and headed down Ninety-Seven toward Annapolis. He wanted Misty here with him now, to tell him everything would be OK. She was always the one to put him at ease in stressful times—when work got demanding and its balance with life seemed unmanageable—and this was the worst it had ever been. He considered calling to ask her to fly out and meet him, but he would be home in only a couple of days. Besides, he, the craftsman, and the craftsman's apprentice were the only three people to have laid eyes on the yacht yet, and even upon his own latest viewing he had seen little more than the black locust frame and the shipments of lumber that had just arrived from Burma and Mozambique. Grey had imagined Misty's first sight of it as a joyous and climactic moment before their first sail. The current circumstances were not so, and he knew that if she were here with him she would be unable to resist a glimpse.

He left the car with the valet at the Westin and checked into his room, finally able to cleanse himself of the reek of Italian food and alcohol and get into a fresh change of clothes. Grey felt like a new man in old jeans and a t-shirt.

He took his suit to the front desk and left it to be dry-cleaned, debating whether he would ever return to collect it. That suit would always remind him of the night when everything had come crashing down, the catastrophic consequences of which he still had yet to comprehend.

He boarded the Circulator Trolley just outside the hotel and rode down West Street, around Church Circle and onto Main Street, watching the dome and spire of the Maryland State House pass in the background of historic Annapolis. He stepped off at the roundabout at Ego Alley and walked to the boathouse where he was to meet the master craftsman whom he and Misty had commissioned and view the realized product of his first nautical design.

"Grey! It's been too long!" exclaimed the craftsman as the visitor came through the door to the two-man workshop he operated with his son.

"Ankur, it's good to see you."

"I'm so excited you're here! Grab a beer; the fridge is over there. Let me show you what we've got."

The refrigerator was stocked with craft beers from all over the world. Grey chose one of Ankur's own brews, an unlabeled amber ale that he had been perfecting for years, changing the recipe just slightly each time. The craftsman was never quite satisfied that a piece of work—a piece of art—was complete. These two men were similar in that way. Grey recalled the ale from he and Misty's first meeting with Ankur months before, and he knew it would please the craftsman to see the selection he had made. It was indeed even more refined than he remembered.

"Kiel!" Ankur called. "Grey is here. It's time to unveil the vessel."

The boy emerged and raised the roll-up door to let in the afternoon sun, then greeted Grey as he climbed a ladder to the opposite side of the lifted and covered craft from where his father stood. Together they turned back the black sheet, rolling it gently from bow to stern as Grey beheld his masterpiece taking shape before him.

"Beautiful, isn't she?" said Ankur.

Grey was in awe. The yacht was exactly as he had imagined her—a fifty-foot sloop with a rich teak hull and decking, African blackwood gunwales and trim, copper hardware, and porthole windows lining half her length on either side from the bow to the shallow vee stern. Her beam was narrow to minimize drag in the wind and water, thereby maximizing her capacity for speed. The cabin contained a single large berth fore, oversized cold storage and head aft, and a central galley and large living compartment designed with materials to compliment her beautiful, sleek, and minimalistic exterior. The cabin ceiling was lined down the center with butterfly hatches to bring the inside out and the outside in, merging the two worlds into one. Wright would be proud, he thought.

It felt natural to refer to her as feminine now, with all the care and love Grey had devoted to her, and would continue to, till death do them part. Misty had left the responsibility of naming the yacht to him, as she had contributed to many components of the endeavor but all along considered the project Grey's baby. Though he had as yet kept it secret, he had chosen a name as a tribute to Misty for whom he had designed the vessel to emulate her natural and eternal beauty—her warm, smooth surfaces and soft curves.

"What will you call her," asked Ankur.

"*Mistical Reflection*," Grey smiled, never taking his eyes off of her.

He walked slowly along her perimeter, examining every square inch, running his fingers down the seamless carvel planking of her glossy hull, the glistening sun streaking along her brightwork with every step he took. Leaving his shoes on the shop floor, he climbed the stairs to look over the deck, the subtle camber reaching its summit at the mast partner. Near the bow, a black onyx and copper compass inlay graced the decking, mirroring another that doubled as a hatch for access to the inboard engine at the helm. The finishing touch was her vintage wheel, salvaged from a Caribbean shipwreck.

She was a work of art so beautiful that Grey hesitated to burden her with his own weight, but under his feet her deck felt more solid than any floor upon which he had ever stood. He stepped down into the cabin where the rich natural tones took his breath away. The deep teak of her bulkheads flowed into the furniture and galley. The berth and seat cushions, upholstered in black diamond tuck leather, were exactly as Misty had specified, as were the stainless galley appliances and the bright red antique doors with colorful rope pulls emulating those of an ancient Tibetan monastery. Usonian sconces that she had designed herself alternated between the portholes, bringing a warm, natural glow to each compartment.

She was distinctive in nearly every way from most modern yachts—particularly most her size—and not only in terms of her construction materials. With just one berth, walk-in cold storage, and a built in water purifier, she was designed for extended voyages occupied by only two sailors. They could, Grey thought, live forever on the open ocean, permanently tied to no singular place. They could go anywhere on earth, relying only on the wind to take them there. Iceland. New Zealand. French Polynesia. The Seychelles. His imagination ran through the list of foreign lands to which he had always dreamt of traveling. Even the remotest of places were within their grasp.

Ankur and Kiel stood by outside the vessel, patiently waiting as Grey studied every surface and every crevice of her, inside and out. The craftsman was grateful to have a client as particular as he himself was. Most of his commissions since emigrating from India to Germany, and then Germany to the United States, were ordered by wealthy clients, or the people of wealthy clients, who scrutinized only superficially upon completion and never fully appreciated the true artistic meaning and significance of the crafts they had purchased. Of the dozens of yachts around the world revitalized or built from scratch by Ankur, and now Kiel, they both knew that this was truly one of their finest.

"What do you think?" asked Ankur when Grey emerged from the cabin, though he already knew the answer.

"She's perfect," Grey replied. "I have to call Misty, then I'm taking you two out for dinner to celebrate."

He stepped outside and tapped the first name on his speed dial. Misty answered immediately, panting.

"Tell me! Tell me!" she demanded.

Grey heard the distinct creak of the back door to their house closing. "Are you OK?" he asked.

"I'm fine. Just got back from a run. Tell me about our boat!"

"You won't believe it. I can't wait for you to see her."

"Did they get the sconces right?"

"They got everything right."

"I want to come out and see her!"

"Soon," he said. "Soon."

"Well, our workload just got a lot lighter. We have the time now."

"Yes, we do."

Grey left Ankur and Kiel, and on the trolley headed back to his hotel he made reservations for the three of them at The Narrows that evening. Of all the Maryland crab cakes he had sampled, theirs were the best he had ever tasted, and he could never pass up the scarce opportunity to enjoy them again. He expected, though, that those opportunities would become more frequent now that he and Misty had ample reason to make the trip to Annapolis. This would be the *Mistical Reflection's* berth.

Over dinner they discussed the yacht's maiden voyage, which Grey had planned for two weeks later as a surprise for Misty. Still overcome with the joy of the afternoon, it only briefly crossed his mind that the day prior had been one of the strangest and worst of his life. Such a professional setback, although profound, was perhaps not enough to spoil all of the things that he and Misty still had going for them. After all, they still had each other, and they were both equally to blame. The next day he would do his best to forget it all as he and Ankur reviewed the plans one final time and scoured the craft for any minor flaw or missed detail. Then the following morning he would drive back to Baltimore and fly home.

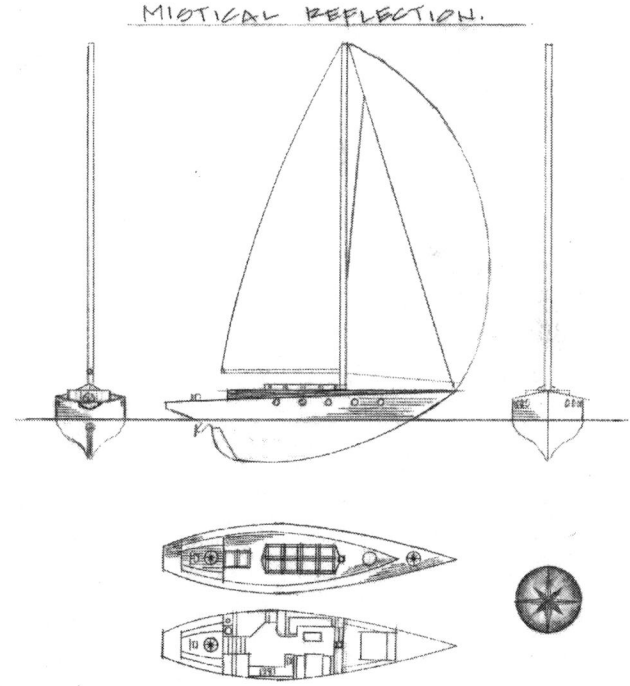

# 4

## Tuesday

Despite her composure on the phone, Misty was distraught when she hung up after talking to Grey on Tuesday morning. They had worked so hard to build this beautiful thing together, and it was as if everything they had done—the all-night work sessions, last minute change orders, the strange rules and secrecy they had tried their best to honor—all meant nothing to the developer. It was unfathomable that anyone could take something so precious from two dedicated artists simply because they happened to fall in love, and it drove her into a rage.

Misty did have one simple remedy to burn her Irish fury in times like this; she would run. Of all the things she had to lose, they could not take the freedom of her feet on the road, never running away from the things by which she was driven, but always toward the obstacles that stood in her way. And she would never stop until she had conquered them. If Misty had taught Grey one thing it was that the best way to see her succeed at anything was to tell her it was impossible.

She slipped on her running shoes with last month's marathon tracker still wrapped through the laces, tied up her hair, stepped outside onto the driveway, and slammed the door behind her. It was getting harder to close as the jamb warped in the cooling weather and changing humidity. The first snow of the season stuck to the pink fabric of her jacket as it fell. She scrolled through the *Run and Dance* playlist on her iPod to find the perfect song and then hit the road without taking a moment to stretch, plan a route, or consider her pace.

Colors of fire and ice in the trees lined the streets of Kirkwood, its picturesque historic homes seeming even more beautiful behind the contrast of blending seasons. Unlit Jack-o'-Lanterns on front porches glared at her with their dark, vacant eyes. Eerie smiles grew on the faces of scarecrows that silently screamed of looming disaster that was yet equally silent in Misty's subconscious. She followed Lockwood through Webster Groves then turned north to Brentwood and onto busier streets.

The tall buildings of Clayton, St. Louis's second skyline, emerged beneath the gray sky as she headed toward the city. Sounds of traffic on the roads around her were silenced by her earbuds and replaced with her own soundtrack, as if the beats she heard were produced by the impact of her feet on the pavement and the music by the fluid movement of every muscle in her body. Her heart raced with the same rhythmic consistency of her breath.

Misty cut through neighborhoods of elegant old mansions that ceased at the western edge of Forest Park, and then she followed the trail beneath falling leaves and snow past the St. Louis Art Museum with its grand Ancient Roman presence looming over Art Hill and the basin below. She ran past the zoo, then the Muny theatre and architectural remnants from the 1904 World's Fair. She had run miles and miles, and yet her feet kept moving her across the park's rolling hills. At Kingshighway the city suddenly appeared again. She passed the Art Deco tower of the Chase Park Plaza and the iconic Neo-Byzantine and Romanesque Revival dome and spires of the Cathedral Basilica in the Central West End, then beneath the SLU seal between its brick columns and through the university campus with the Gateway Arch ahead in the distance. It was not until she saw Union Station and the site of the partially erected Star Silo that she stopped.

Misty paused the music as she stood outside the fence that bordered the site. A banner hung there with Grey's rendering of the future building, and she looked up at the web of steel beams and columns hundreds of feet in the air. She imagined that one day it might represent the history of this city alongside all of the beautiful buildings she had passed on the way, and she hoped that its secrets would not forever haunt its legacy. Someday, she thought, those secrets would be forgotten by everyone but she and Grey.

But what were those secrets? As she stood gazing at the skilled men traversing the metal skeleton, working diligently to see the design through to fruition, she began to wonder not only about the ominous mystery that surrounded it, but also about the implications of her involvement, Grey's involvement, and their involvement with each other. She wondered if he knew more than he was letting on, and if he did, why he would not tell her. Was he now concerned for her safety? Certainly, she thought, he would never knowingly put her in danger.

A chill ran through her at the thought of Grey's suspicion that someone had been watching them. She licked the salt from her lips and looked around at the cars and people passing by, wondering if any of them had followed her here. Nothing looked out of the ordinary, but she was not used to watching for hunters. She started the music again and headed west to retrace her route, following the trail of her own footsteps in the thin layer of snow.

When Misty finally reached their driveway she looked down at her phone. It had been almost five hours since she had stepped out the door that morning, and the mileage indicator on her route-tracking app exceeded a marathon. Just as she was reaching for the door, Grey's face appeared on the screen and she answered, still panting.

Misty felt better after talking to Grey. His voice always had a way of putting her at ease. She poured a glass of chocolate almond milk as her runner's high settled and stepped carefully up the stairs with quivering legs. Her breath was still heavy as she ran a hot bath, peeled off her sodden clothes, and slipped into the tub. She washed the perspired salt from her hair, her skin absorbing the Epsom salt in the water. Subtle, rhythmic ripples appeared at the surface with each beat of her heart until her body finally relaxed. She lay there for a while before getting out of the bath, drying off, slipping naked into the silky sheets of their bed, and falling asleep.

# 5

## The Interview

Things got strange again as soon as Grey got off the plane at Lambert around noon on Thursday. He stepped out of the jet bridge at the airport terminal gate and immediately noticed two more suited men, one near his father's age and one around his own, rising from their seats as if to collect a passenger from the flight. Both were clean-shaven, almost military in their posture, but maintaining a professional presence. They seemed cold—emotionless. Though not as expensively attired as Mancini's men in Chicago, there was something eerie and discomforting about the way they seemed to watch him. Grey made an effort to avoid eye contact as he walked past them through Concourse C.

When he reached the main terminal he stopped and took his phone from his pocket as if to make a call, stepping aside to see if the two men were following him. He put it to his ear, listening to silence as he glanced carefully over his shoulder. If they were there for him, he wondered whether they would dare approach him in such a public place, or if perhaps they planned to follow him home. They drifted past among the crowd, apparently engaged in their own business, and he waited until they were out of sight to put his phone away and continue on.

He stopped at Starbucks for a coffee, discreetly eyeing his surroundings, and sat at a table for a moment to let his racing heart settle. The sounds of hurried travelers and flight announcements clashed against the trendy, upbeat music playing in the café. He had already been fired from the job, and he wondered what more they could want from him. It was possible that his imagination and suspicions surrounding the Mancini situation were getting the better of him, but his gut told him otherwise. He thought back to the conversation with his father on Sunday. *Be careful.* It was becoming clear to Grey that there was more to this man and the Star Silo project than he knew, and he whispered to himself, "What did I get us into?" He took a breath and rose from his seat, tossing the half-empty coffee into the garbage can beside him, and headed toward the escalator to the lower level.

Grey peered between the columns and people waiting for their luggage at the baggage claim carousel, but there was no sign of the two men. He watched his bag ejected from the carousel hatch and let it circle a few times, waiting for them to reappear. It seemed they were no longer following him, if they had been at all. One by one, bags were collected and travelers dispersed until the carousel stopped, leaving his lone suitcase waiting unclaimed. "You're paranoid," he said to himself, and he picked up his bag and walked calmly toward the parking garage.

Just as he passed through the automatic doors to the garage, he saw them again, standing in the shadows at a distance from the door. As they turned toward him, Grey noticed the bulge beneath the younger man's jacket, and both began to move in his direction. Taking the parking tag from his pocket, he walked quickly toward the section where his car was supposed to be parked, weaving his way through the lot to lose the tail. He could hear their footsteps smacking the pavement as briskly as his own. As soon as he saw his car he began to run. He yanked the door open, jumped in, threw his bags into the passenger seat, and sped through the garage toward the exit, too terrified to even glance back at the pair of men chasing him.

On the highway, Grey thought he had lost them. He looked constantly in the rear view mirror, watching for any conspicuous-looking vehicle—any black luxury sedan with tinted windows driving fast enough to keep up. Just to be safe he took a route fifteen minutes out of the way winding through neighborhood streets. There was no chance that anyone still following him could go unnoticed. He could not take the risk of leading these people directly to his own front door, though with their resources it was unlikely that they did not already have his home address. The thought that he and Misty were not even safe in their own house sickened him.

Grey rolled slowly into the driveway. He turned off the car and sat in silence for a moment before gathering his bags from the seat beside him and getting out. As he headed across the front walk toward the door, a black Ford sedan pulled up to the curb in front of his house. He stopped in his tracks as the two men from the airport stepped out and began to approach him. His eyes drifted up and down the street, then to his car, and back at the men on his front lawn, and his stomach sank as the older man reached around to his back.

"Mr. Cavanaugh," said the man, bringing his hand back to produce not a gun, but a set of credentials and a gold badge, "I'm Special Agent McGuinness. This is Special Agent Richter. We're with the FBI. We'd like to talk with you. May we come inside?"

"The FBI?" asked Grey. "About what?"

"Why don't we talk inside?"

"Alright," he said reluctantly.

His hands were trembling as he took his keys from his pocket and unlocked the door. Agents McGuinness and Richter followed him through the foyer and into the kitchen, were Misty was waiting and threw her arms around him. "I missed you," she said. "Everything is going to be OK."

She jumped back when she saw the two unexpected visitors.

"Misty," said Grey, "these men are with the FBI."

"What?"

"Miss Sommer," said McGuinness, "we have a situation that we need to discuss with Mr. Cavanaugh." He and Richter politely introduced themselves.

"I don't understand," she said. "Why are you here?"

Richter requested a glass of water, and he and Misty remained in the kitchen as Grey and McGuinness headed into the living room, sitting across from one another.

"OK, Agent McGuinness," said Grey, "what's going on?"

"You can call me Conrad. May I call you Grey?"

"Sure."

"Alright, Grey," he began, unbuttoning his jacket, "we've got some questions about your dealings in Chicago."

Grey scoffed and shook his head. "So do I," he said.

"What do you mean?"

"Nothing. Go on."

"OK, why don't you start by telling me what you were doing up there."

Grey proceeded to give McGuinness a play-by-play of the strange events three days before and the history of the Star Silo project as the agent sat listening, silently and attentively. When Richter and Misty did not join them, he wondered what they were talking about in the kitchen—what he was asking her, and what she was telling him. Grey glanced nervously toward the next room. It dawned on him that the two agents had separated them for a reason: to compare their stories and see how they matched up.

"So, anyway, now Misty and I are going to take a long vacation and put all this behind us."

"Where to?" asked McGuinness.

"Don't know yet," Grey told a half-truth. Though they may not have chosen an exact destination, he knew they would be sailing from Annapolis.

"So you don't remember anything between the time you left the club and the next morning?"

"No." said Grey. "And I'm off the project now, so if you've got questions about that you should talk to Mancini himself. I signed a strict confidentiality agreement."

"That's why I'm here, Grey. We can't talk to Mancini."

"Why not?"

"Because he's dead."

"What?" Grey's stomach dropped again.

"Salvatore Mancini was found Tuesday morning with seventeen stab wounds and his throat cut."

"Oh my God."

"So you say Monday was the first time you'd met him?"

"Yes. Wait, why is the FBI investigating a murder and not the Chicago Police?"

"We're investigating a connection between the murder and organized crime."

"What? Organized crime?"

"Surely you know who you were working for."

"I trust my clients. I don't have any reason to look into their affairs."

"Well you did with this one. Let me fill you in, since I'm sure you were too young to remember the trial. Salvatore Mancini became one of the biggest names in organized crime after he took control of the family business in the late seventies. In nineteen ninety-one he was convicted on multiple racketeering charges including bribery, extortion, and money laundering and sentenced to thirty years in federal prison. He was accused of ordering, and possibly even personally committing, at least twenty-two murders, but he was found not guilty on those charges after three key witnesses disappeared. He was released in two thousand eleven after serving twenty years of his sentence. Since then he had been rebuilding his empire from Chicago, acting as a silent partner in numerous ventures across the country that, on the surface, appeared legitimate. Your project, the Star Silo, was one of those ventures."

Grey wiped the sweat from his face.

"This is insane."

"Did he threaten you in any way?" McGuinness asked. "Maybe threaten your family?"

"No, he just fired us."

"You're sure?"

"Yes."

"OK. I know we didn't give you a chance to unpack. Would you mind letting us take a look at your luggage?"

"Wait, you think I did this?"

"I'll give it to you straight; here's what we know. You were one of the last people seen with him the night he died, and witnesses saw you being dragged out of the club after an argument. You can't tell me what happened after that or how you got back to the Fairmont. The lobby cameras show you stumbling in hours later, apparently very drunk. We found blood in the sink and on the sheets from your hotel room. We're running a DNA comparison. You missed your flight from St. Louis to Chicago, but the next day you were on the flight from Chicago to Baltimore."

"I told you, the guy on the phone said the flight was canceled, and they put me on a private plane."

"We'll look into flight records," said McGuinness, "but none of this looks good. And we know that Mancini specifically asked for you for this job, yet you say you had never met him before and knew nothing about his business."

"I can't explain that either, but everything I've told you is the truth. What are you hoping to find in my bags?"

"Look, Grey, a lot of people wanted this guy dead. We're just going down the list. You can help me cross your name off of it."

"I don't think so. Not without a warrant."

Grey stood up and went for the kitchen.

"Misty, don't say anything else. Agent Richter, you and Agent McGuinness need to leave."

"Grey, what's going on?" Misty demanded.

"We're done talking to them." He pointed to the door. "You can see yourselves out."

McGuinness left his business card on the kitchen table, and the two agents made their way to the door. The whole house seemed to heat up as Richter opened it and the afternoon sunlight burst abrasively into the foyer. Before they left, Agent McGuinness turned to Grey. "Why don't you hold off on that vacation," he said. "We'll be talking again soon. I hope you'll call me first."

When the door closed, Grey kicked off his shoes and threw his jacket over the back of the sofa, then walked to the bar and furiously poured himself a glass of scotch. The bottle rattled against the glass as his hand shook.

He went to the front window and peered through the blinds to be sure that McGuinness and Richter had gone, gulping down the first glass. Then he poured a second. Misty's muffled voice clouded the thoughts racing through his head, demanding answers that he did not have.

"I don't know what to tell you," he said. "I saw them at the airport, then they came here."

"That guy Robert, Agent Richter, whatever, he asked what I knew about Chicago."

"What did you tell him?"

"What could I tell him? I don't know anything."

"Good," said Grey, taking a drink. "We need to get a lawyer. They're trying to pin Mancini's murder on me."

"Why would they do that?"

"They said there was blood in my hotel room. I think someone may be trying to set me up."

"Why you?"

"That's what I'd like to know."

Grey noticed Wednesday's newspaper on the kitchen counter and picked it up. On the front page was a photo of Salvatore Mancini and a headline reading "Mob Boss Found Murdered."

"Did you not see this?"

"You know I don't read the newspaper," Misty replied.

He flipped to the full article. The FBI, it said, was looking into a person of interest with connections to organized crime. Within the same paragraph, it mentioned the Star Silo project. One person of interest. One project.

"Misty, read this," he said, handing her the paper and pointing to that damning paragraph. She looked at it for a moment, then back up at him.

"They can't mean you, right?"

"Who else could they be talking about?"

She shook her head, dumbstruck, as he gulped down the rest of his scotch.

"I need a shower," he said.

Grey picked up his luggage and briefcase on the way upstairs and dropped them in the bedroom before turning on the shower. He left his clothes in a pile on the bathroom floor. He wanted to burn them, like the filthy suit he had left at the hotel in Annapolis. Never in his life had he felt so violated. The authorities, in which he had always placed his faith and trust, had come to his home and accused him of a heinous crime without any real evidence against him. Everything they had was circumstantial, he thought, and not a moment of it was his fault. Even worse, though his name had not yet been released, the media was already reporting on him and making the same wild accusations. He feared that soon every person in America would know his name and face. He wondered what sort of picture they would paint. Would he be a victim of a ruthless criminal enterprise who struck back in self-defense, or would he be a cold-blooded killer?

The whole spectacle in Chicago suddenly made sense. It was no wonder they made such an effort to ensure that he had not been followed and his whereabouts were kept secret. Salvatore Mancini, the mob boss, as Grey now knew him, even in death had managed to place him in a more dangerous situation than he yet knew. Certainly the FBI understood the mob's capabilities—their capacity to drag an innocent man into the criminal underworld against his will. They were just fishing. He could not help but remind himself of the irony that this whole web of horrific events had transpired from his profound love for Misty.

The showerhead whispered as steam filled the bathroom, and Grey inhaled and exhaled deep breaths of the honeysuckle aroma of his bar soap. Tomorrow they would have a real lead, he thought. Agents Conrad McGuinness and Robert Richter would realize his innocence, and this would all be over. Perhaps he might even reclaim his position on the Star Silo project, though he wondered if, given the opportunity, he would even take it back now. He cringed at the thought of profiting from a death, particularly one he was being accused of causing. Looking back, the whole experience had been suspicious from the outset, and the taste of this venture had grown increasingly sour. Perhaps it was time to move on either way.

"Grey!" he heard in the terrified tone of Misty's voice. He slid open the shower door, and through the steam he saw a matching look on her face as she stood with his blood-soaked button down shirt in one hand and a knife in the other.

"What the hell?" he demanded. "Are you OK? Did you cut yourself?"

"These were in your suitcase."

He turned off the shower and stepped out to look more closely.

"The knife too?"

"Yes. I was going to do your laundry."

"This doesn't make sense," he said. "This shirt was clean when I packed it this morning, and that's not my knife."

She stepped back and looked at him.

"You don't think I actually had something to do with a murder," said Grey, "do you?"

"Of course not," she said. "But how did this happen?"

He took the bloody shirt and knife from her, staring at them in his hands in utter bewilderment.

"Well, we have to call those FBI guys," said Misty.

"Are you kidding? Someone is obviously trying to frame me, and for all I know they're behind it. Those guys were at the airport waiting for me when I got off the plane, so they knew I was on that flight."

"Why didn't you talk to them then?"

"I didn't know who they were. I was trying to get away from them."

"You ran from the FBI?"

"I didn't know they were FBI!" Grey yelled at her. "I thought they worked for Mancini."

"Well how do you think this looks now, Grey?"

"What was I supposed to do?"

Misty had no answer. She had not been with Grey in Chicago, and she had not experienced the fear he had felt then or even the same he felt now. She tried to put herself in his shoes, but the whole situation was so surreal and ludicrous that neither of them could ever have been prepared for it. Honest people are never put in such positions, she thought.

"Let's just call them," she said. "Maybe it isn't even Salvatore Mancini's blood."

"You think someone would go through all this to plant fake blood? No way. We can't trust anyone."

"There's one person we can trust," said Misty.

"Who?"

"Your father. He always seems to have an answer."

Just then the phone began to ring.

# 6

## Declan's Secrets

"Dad," said Grey when he picked up the phone.
"Grey, I heard about Mancini. Are you and Misty OK?"

"I wish I could say yes. The FBI was just here—"

"Don't say anything else," Declan interrupted. "I'll be at your house in an hour."

The line went dead. The tone in his father's voice was one Grey had heard only once before—on Sunday, at the mention of the name of he and Misty's recently departed employer. He tried to call back, to demand an explanation for this brief and unnerving exchange, but there was no answer.

Grey dressed and began pacing the room as Misty sat on the bed with her face in her hands. He watched the clock on the wall, its second hand echoing in his ears with each advance. Every second ticked by with a new possibility of its own, and every minute that passed felt like hours. This feeling of helplessness was foreign to both of them. Misty began to cry, and he knew that this time it was she who needed reassurances, even if he had no real answers or truth to tell. He sat on the bed beside her and put his arm around her, and her head fell to his shoulder.

"We're going to be fine, baby," he said. "We can get through anything."

Such was their way. Whenever he would fall, she would be there to lift him up again, and he was there to do the same for her. As long as they were together, they could accomplish anything they could dream up and overcome any tribulation with which they were faced. The mob, the FBI, the world had nothing on them. It was Grey's turn to be strong for Misty, and he closed his eyes and took a breath, waiting and listening to the monotonous tick—tick—tick of the clock.

A knock came at the back door. Misty wiped her eyes as she and Grey headed out of the bedroom and back downstairs. Grey saw his father's car parked on the rear entry driveway and went to the door to unlock it. Declan swiftly came inside with a duffel bag in his hand and locked the door again behind him.

"Has anyone else come to see you?" he asked.

"No," said Grey. "Why?"

"Good," he replied, dropping the duffel bag on the kitchen counter.

"What's going on," Misty demanded.

"I'm sure by now you know who Mancini was," said Declan, unzipping the bag, "and you know the FBI is on to you."

"But I didn't do anything," Grey insisted.

"That doesn't matter to the mob. Mancini's men will be coming here, and you'd better be gone when they arrive."

He threw the flap of the bag open and began removing items and setting them on the counter, starting with two Nebraska license plates.

"That boat you've been building, is it finished?"

"Yes."

"Good," said Declan. "They'll know your car, so you'll take mine. These plates are clean. If you get stopped by a cop they'll come back to your new identity."

"What are you talking about?" asked Grey.

Declan removed two new passports and drivers licenses with Grey and Misty's photos on them and the names Stephen Johnson and Melissa Cruise, rubber banded with a stack of matching credit cards.

"I need both of your wallets," he said.

"Why?" asked Grey.

"We don't have time for questions right now," Declan insisted. "Just get them."

Misty ran to the bedroom and brought back both of their wallets, which Declan emptied, replacing the cards inside with the new ones he had brought. Then, from the bag he removed a new cell phone, a satellite phone, and an index card full of typed numbers and letters.

"This is a list of bank account numbers, all in your new names. The acronyms correspond to banks based in the US, Cayman Islands, and Switzerland, just in case anyone catches on. You've got plenty of money to get by until this is sorted out."

"Dad!" Grey yelled, slamming his fist on the counter. "What the hell are you talking about? Where did you get this stuff?"

"It doesn't matter where it came from," Declan calmly replied. "All that matters is that you listen to me, because if you don't, you're dead. The mob is after you because they think you killed Mancini, and when—not if—when the FBI arrests you, it'll be even easier for them to get to you. Right now you have one option."

"What's that?"

"You run. Fast. Get out of town, get to that boat, and get on the ocean where they can't track you. Don't tell anyone where you're going. You can communicate with me, and only me, using this satphone. We'll talk more later, but right now you have to go. You've got ten minutes to pack this bag with whatever you need. Misty, I've got a safe house set up where you can lay low for a while."

"What?" she asked.

"You can't stay here. They'll use you to get to Grey."

"No. Wherever Grey is going, I'm going with him."

"Misty," said Grey, "he's right. You're not safe with me now."

"And you think I'm safer alone? You think you are? I'm not going anywhere without you. We can move faster sailing together, and we can protect each other."

"Misty—"

"No. That's the way it is."

"Alright," said Declan. "Maybe it's better this way. Let's get going."

He handed them the duffel bag and went outside to change the license plates on the BMW as Grey and Misty bolted up the stairs. Neither spoke a word as they dashed between their dressers, the closet, and the bathroom to collect every necessary item they could think of. The second hand on the clock that only minutes before had tortured Grey with its mind-numbing tedium was now racing against the beats of his heart. Every time he passed by the door to the bathroom, its yellow lights and white tile drawing his eye to that macabre scene on the floor, his stomach sickened. The bloody white shirt and black knife would forever in his mind serve as symbols for one life lost and two more in ruin, and he could not help but wonder what his father had to do with all of this. How could a simple civil engineer from the Midwest know the things he seemed to know?

In ten minutes they were back downstairs with Declan.

"Are you ready?" he asked.

"Dad, there's a bloody shirt and knife upstairs from my bag. I don't know what to do with them."

"Don't worry about that," Declan replied with no trace of surprise in his voice. "I'll take care of it."

They went out to Declan's car in the driveway and threw the bag in the trunk. Grey and Misty looked up at their home for a moment before getting in, wondering if they would ever be able to live there again.

"Alright," said Declan, leaning down to Grey's window, "now, you'll drive straight through the night. You should get to Annapolis shortly before sunrise. Grey, if you get tired, Misty, you drive so he can sleep. Do not stop for any reason other than to fill up on gas. Follow speed limits and don't do anything to get stopped by the police. When you get there, leave my car at the Noah Hillman Parking Garage, then use the satphone to call me once you're out of the Chesapeake and on the Atlantic. My number is the first on speed dial. I'll have the car picked up before anyone catches on."

"We'll have to call Ankur on the way," said Grey. "To get the boat ready."

"Alright. Make sure he doesn't tell anyone you're coming. Misty, let your family know you're going on a long vacation and will be out of touch for a while. We don't want them going to the police. But make it brief, and only one call. The FBI won't have them tapped yet, but it won't be long. Use the cell phone, and toss it when you're through. We can get you a new burner later. After today, no calls to anyone but me."

"When can we come home?" asked Misty.

"That will depend on a lot of things," said Declan. "I'm going to get to the bottom of this; you just need to trust me." He looked at Grey. "I'll do whatever I have to do to clear your name."

"Thank you."

"Now get out of here."

# 7

## 2222 Market Street

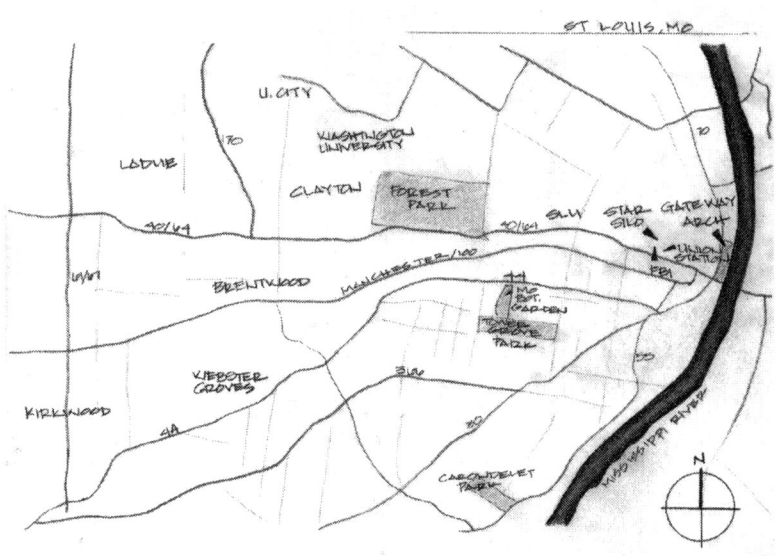

     Agent McGuinness gazed out the window of his office at the St. Louis division of the FBI toward the Star Silo frame across the street. Each day since commencement he had watched it evolve and grow, resembling more and more the magnificent rendering on the banner that faced Market Street. He had looked forward to the revival of the barren parking lot that tarnished his view of this once beautiful and thriving city. Perhaps this single building, he thought, could mark the turning point in the downward spiral that had plagued the city's culture and economy for years. He had grown up in St. Louis, and though his work had taken him to dozens of cities and burned through two marriages throughout the course of his career, he had finally returned to the place that had always been his home.

"He's definitely lying," said Richter, leaning over the partition that separated their cubicles.

"I don't know," McGuinness replied.

"What, really?"

"The guy had no idea what I was talking about. I don't think he did it. He's an architect, not a mobster."

"Under the right circumstances, anyone can become a killer. You know, when I requested to be assigned to this office I was hoping to learn from you, but for a guy they still teach courses on at Quantico you're pretty quick to drop a lead."

"Sure, when it's a bad lead."

"I'm just saying maybe you've been doing this job too long, Connie."

"You haven't been doing it long enough to be so cynical, Rob. Sometimes people are innocent."

"Nobody's innocent."

McGuinness shook his head and looked out the window again. He wondered if Richter had heard that in a movie or something. Maybe it was just the attitude of a newbie with dual degrees in criminal justice and accounting and high enough test scores to be hired as a special agent with no actual police or fieldwork under his belt. But perhaps Richter was right. In his twenty-five years on the job, not including those spent with the St. Louis Metropolitan Police force before, McGuinness had grown sympathetic to those unfortunate souls caught in the crosshairs of the FBI, particularly his own. He had set the standard for interrogation tactics. Not so long ago he had been just like Richter, always assuming the worst in people. Perhaps time had softened his approach. He had his doubts about whether his career success had been worth everything he had sacrificed for the job. Maybe he had been too easy on Grey.

"Look out there," McGuinness pointed out the window toward the site of the Star Silo. "Why would a guy who can do that kill a mob boss?"

"Why not?" Richter shrugged.

"Grey is too methodical and controlled to commit such a sloppy crime and leave so much evidence. It's just too easy."

"Grey? You're on a first name basis with our suspect?"

"I know him."

"You know him?"

"I mean I knew his—I know guys like this. Like you said, I've been doing this a long time."

"I said you've been doing it too long. You and—what's her name? Your lady in Chicago who passed this case on to us."

"Carla Sanborn. We worked together a long time ago. And it's not like she just dumped it on us. They're working their end, and I offered to help out with the Cavanaugh angle since he's here in town."

"Anyway, hypothetically, even if he didn't kill Mancini, which he did, we know he's involved in some weird shit. You saw the building plans."

"Maybe," replied McGuinness.

"How much did you tell him anyway?"

"Just what I had to."

"Well, now he's spooked," said Richter. "We'll be lucky if he doesn't run. Look, you're less than a year from mandatory retirement. Let me have a shot. Next time I'll talk to him, and you can talk to the girl."

"Sure."

"Hey, I'm making a sacrifice for you, old timer. She's nice to look at—sexy and professional all in one. That body, and those eyes—those eyes tell it all, man. I bet she's wild in the—"

"Alright, alright. Shut up and get to work. If you're so sure Cavanaugh is good for it then let's stick with the lead. I'll look into flight records out of Spirit. You book us a flight to Baltimore. I want to check out that hotel he stayed at in Annapolis and figure out what he was doing there."

# 8

## On the Run

Misty fought back tears as they traveled east on Highway Forty and the St. Louis skyline grew. She envisioned how it would one day look with the Star Silo casting its shadow eastward down the north side of Market Street at this time of day, the contemporary tower beautifully juxtaposed with the classic Romanesque architecture of Union Station just a block away. From the Illinois side it would be a soaring centerpiece beneath the Gateway Arch at a distance behind the Old Courthouse, and from the west it would appear on approach as the tallest structure in the city.

She imagined the sunlight beaming into the rooms she had designed through the walls of windows that wrapped the building, the way the colors and rich wood tones would glow so naturally. Misty had hoped that one day she and Grey could have an office of their own within this beautiful work of art they had created together. They made a perfect team, she thought. A union of their two small businesses was only a matter of time, like the union of their hands in marriage. They had briefly discussed both, but it was unanimously decided that it would be best to wait until this project was complete before taking on any more big commitments like a merger or wedding planning. Now she wondered if either was still in the cards.

"Hello?" Ankur's voice came through the car speakers.

"Ankur, it's Grey. Change of plan. I need you to put the boat in the water and raise the mast."

"Grey? I thought you went home."

"I did. Misty and I are on our way back. We'll be in Annapolis early tomorrow morning, probably before sunrise. I'm sorry for the short notice, but we're in quite a hurry. We'll also need it stocked with food so that we can set sail immediately."

"Why the rush?"

"I'll explain when we get there, just trust me. And it's very important that you don't mention to anyone that we're coming."

"You got it. I like working on the water by the moonlight anyway."

The sun fell slowly behind them as they moved east, the orange glow inside the car gradually fading to gray, then black, lit only by the dials on the dashboard, the headlights of passing cars, and the moon. Under that same moon Ankur and Kiel were preparing for Grey and Misty their getaway, unwise to the fact that they were effectively aiding and abetting two people who would likely be called fugitives tomorrow. Misty felt guilty bringing them into this mess, but there was no other choice. She leaned the seat back and tried to sleep, her thoughts racing behind her eyelids, wondering where she and Grey would go and if they were really safe anywhere. She listened to him shuffling in the driver's seat, trying to find a comfortable position over the subtle, droning hum of the Bavarian engine. She wondered what he was thinking now—if he had considered a course. Perhaps they would sail north toward Greenland, or east toward Europe. The former would leave them isolated, and too easy to find amongst a population comparable to that of a medium-sized American municipality. The latter, she feared, may place them out of the reach of the FBI as they fell right into the palms of Mancini's cronies in Italy. She had read *The Godfather*, but never did she expect that it would hit so close to home. She imagined places even more distant, more remote, but perhaps there were nearer options south that would leave them less vulnerable.

Sleepless hours passed without a word spoken. Misty figured they were somewhere near Columbus as the sounds of traffic picked up and the backs of her eyelids glowed orange. She sat up and looked at Grey.

"I can drive if you want. You need to sleep."

"So do you."

"I have been."

"Liar," he smiled.

"Hey—"

He looked at her.

"—I love you."

"I love you more. I'll stop for gas once we get through the city. Then we can switch."

"OK," she said. "Where do you think we'll go?"

"I don't know."

"What about the Caribbean? Hundreds of islands, tourists are common and US currency is accepted. If we have to move, we can quickly sail to another island under a different government and law enforcement."

"Yeah, maybe."

Misty turned up the heat and rubbed her dry palms together, looking at the empty ring finger on her left hand. These people had taken everything from her—everything except for Grey. Her job. Her home. Her sense of peace and freedom. She feared now that even that final and most important piece of her life she still held onto could be stolen away as easily as the rest. Images of handcuffs and guns rolled through her mind, and she wondered which she should fear more.

They stopped at a rural gas station off Interstate Seventy and Misty moved to the driver's seat, watching as Grey filled the tank under the bright, fluorescent lights of the canopy. Once he was back in the car he was asleep before she had even pulled onto the entrance ramp.

Her foot gradually sunk toward the floor as she began to wonder about Grey's innocence. It made no sense for someone to frame him. That sort of thing only happens in books and movies. He was an architect, for God's sake. Of all people to be framed for the murder of a crime boss, certainly he must have been at the bottom of the list of likely candidates.

The purring of the engine increased with such subtlety that she hardly noticed, and she never glanced at the needle on the speedometer. The forests passed by in a blur and headlights shrunk in the rear view mirror as the black mountains of western Maryland grew on either side of the highway, silhouetted by the endless array of stars behind them. She looked at Grey sleeping peacefully beside her, wondering what he was dreaming about. Even as her suspicions grew, she hoped she was a part of his dreams.

Then she thought of Declan. From what Grey had told her, everything about his childhood had seemed normal. His father had been there to cheer at his baseball games, to help him with his algebra homework, to teach him to drive. All he had absorbed from Declan had led Grey to build a respectable career designing skyscrapers that would alter a city skyline for generations. Now Misty was beginning to wonder if anything Grey knew about the man who had raised him was actually true. She wondered how Declan could know everything before they had even told him. Only a certain kind of person could manipulate DOR records and produce false drivers licenses and plates and passports at a moment's notice, and then there were the bank accounts and burner phones. Perhaps an even more chilling thought, it was possible that he had kept these things waiting in anticipation of a time when he knew they would be on the run from the law. Declan had not taken a moment to ask whether Grey was innocent or how he had gotten into this mess. It could have been his love for his son that kept him from asking, but maybe he already knew the answer. Then came the unnerving question of whether Declan was somehow involved.

She looked at Grey again, and the inside of the car lit up blue. Misty's stomach sank and Grey sat up, the sound of the siren ringing in their ears. He turned to look behind them and the spotlight from the police car shone right in his eyes.

"Shit! Shit! Shit!"

"What should I do?"

"You're not going to outrun the police," he said. "Just stay calm. This is what the IDs are for."

She slowed down to pull over as he scrambled to find her wallet in her purse.

"How fast were you going?"

"I don't know."

"OK," he said, handing her the false license of Melissa Cruise. "Look at it. Memorize your birthday and address. We're on our way to New York to visit my family, OK?"

"OK."

The police car followed as she pulled over to the side of the road. She skimmed the license as Grey took out his own to do the same.

> Melissa Cruise
> 4-30-1988
> 4501 Washington Blvd
> Lincoln, NE 68502

Stephen Johnson
2-13-1985
2725 Harrison Ave
Lincoln, NE 68502

They were both still looking down when the cop knocked on Misty's window. She rolled it down.

"I'm Officer Lantz with the Maryland State Police. Do you know why I stopped you this morning, ma'am?"

"Was I driving too fast?"

"Good guess. I clocked you at ninety-two miles an hour."

Grey closed his eyes and shook his head.

"May I see your drivers license and proof of insurance?"

She handed him the license as Grey sifted through the glove compartment for insurance information.

"Where are you headed in such a hurry?"

"I'm sorry, Officer. We're on our way to New York to visit his family."

Grey found the insurance card and handed it to the trooper, suddenly realizing that he had not checked to see if his father had switched it with one that matched his new name. The cop compared the card with Misty's license and then looked up at her.

"Trying to make that drive in one night? Why didn't you stop to sleep?"

"We didn't want to pay for a hotel," said Grey.

Officer Lantz's eyes scanned the new BMW. Then he leaned down and looked through the window with his eyebrows raised at Grey.

"Really?"

"I prefer driving at night," Misty interjected, reaching out and touching the cop's hand. "Less traffic."

"I see," he smiled at her, then looked at Grey again. "Sir, can I get your ID as well?"

Grey's hand was shaking as he handed Officer Lantz the fake.

"Wait here just a minute," said the trooper before turning and walking back to his car. The blue and red lights flashed across the dashboard, and Grey could already feel the cuffs on his wrists and hear the sound of the cell door slamming shut. He hoped that the plates and his new name matched the insurance information, but if the cop was suspicious he might run the VIN. Grey prayed that his father had been thorough enough to cover all of these tracks. He looked at Misty.

"What the hell were you thinking driving so fast?"

"I didn't mean to."

"And why did you touch his hand? Are you crazy?"

"Didn't you see the way he looked at me?" she asked.

"What way?"

"Just trust me."

He looked forward silently and took a breath, his eyes alternating between the side and rear view mirrors. A few minutes later another police cruiser pulled up behind the first with its lights on, and the second trooper got out to talk to Lantz. Both approached the BMW again on opposite sides.

"Step out of the car please, ma'am," said Officer Lantz, then looking at Grey. "You too, sir."

Slowly they both opened their doors and stepped out.

"Put your hands on the roof of the vehicle and spread your feet, please."

They both complied, looking across the roof of the car into each other's eyes as the cops patted them down and searched their pockets.

"Do you have any weapons?" the second trooper asked Grey. "Anything on you that could hurt me?"

"Of course not."

The cop ran his fingers along the inside of Grey's belt, and he wondered if Lantz was doing the same to Misty. He saw the officer whisper into her ear as she stared forward without a sound.

"OK, what the hell is going on?" Grey demanded, taking his hands off the car and turning toward the cop. The trooper jumped back and drew his gun, pointing it at Grey.

"Turn around and put your hands on the car now!"

"You stopped us for speeding! Do we look like criminals to you?"

"Wait," said Lantz, leaving Misty and walking over to the other officer pointing his gun at Grey. They moved out of the sight of the dashboard camera in Lantz's car and spoke briefly and quietly before the trooper holstered his pistol. Lantz walked slowly back to Misty.

"This name has brought you bad luck," he said, handing their IDs and insurance information back to her, "but I'm going to let you go with a warning this time. Try to slow down, Miss Cruise."

Without another word, both troopers went back to their cars, pulled onto the highway, and disappeared. Grey and Misty got back into the BMW.

"What the hell just happened?" Grey asked. "Did he touch you?"

"No," replied Misty, "but he gave me this." She reached into her pocket and pulled out a thick manila envelope. "He said to tell Ankur it's a bonus for his help and his silence."

Grey slid a wad of cash out of the envelope and flipped through the bills.

"Misty, there's a hundred thousand dollars here."

Her eyes widened.

"Your dad?"

"Who else?"

She pulled the car back onto the road and set the cruise control at seventy. By the time they reached Annapolis the stars were dimming with the indigo glow in the east. They left the car at the garage as Declan had instructed and walked with the duffel bag toward Ankur's shop at the water's edge. The door was standing open, and they stepped in to find Ankur and Kiel having breakfast with the roll-up door open to the harbor. Behind them, Grey saw the vessel in the water, rigged and ready to sail.

"Ah, you've returned," said Ankur. "It seems like only yesterday we saw you last."

"Day before yesterday, actually," replied Grey. "Are we good?"

"Oh yes. I'll be sad to see her go, but she's all ready for you."

He led them out to the dock where Misty got her first glimpse of their Bermuda-rigged yacht under the royal blue sky of dawn reflected in the water, accented by rippling streams of yellow dock lights and historic brick buildings and white masts. She was as beautiful as they had both envisioned from the moment they had begun to draw up plans, graced with a delicate fusion of classical and contemporary elements that gave her a character unlike any other vessel on the water. Just at the sight of her, Misty felt immediately at home. She was undoubtedly theirs—hers and Grey's—a representation of their love, like a child they had made together.

"I've affixed her name to the stern," said Ankur. "Just peel off the seal when you're ready."

"You picked a name?" asked Misty, turning to Grey.

"I did," he smiled. "Are you ready to go?"

"I've never been so ready."

"Ankur," said Grey, handing him the manila envelope, "this is for you. Some people are looking for us. If they come around asking questions, please keep our business as quiet as possible."

"Of course."

"And whatever they tell you about me, don't believe them."

"I consider you a friend, Grey. And I trust my friends."

"Thank you, Ankur."

"Oh, and I almost forgot. I built you a couple of gifts to accompany her. A pair of kayaks. A motorized dinghy just didn't really seem like your style. They're already aboard."

Grey and Misty boarded their vessel, untied the knots from the copper cleats, and backed her quietly out into the harbor. They raised the sails and began a southern heading on the Chesapeake just as the sun broke over the eastern horizon.

# 9

# Atlantic

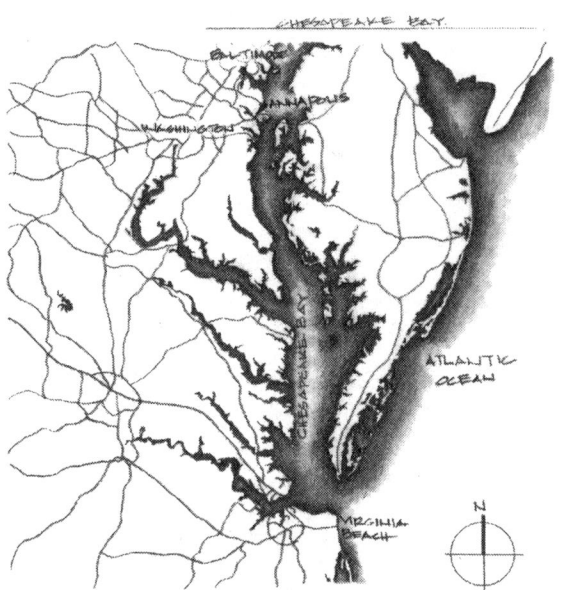

**S**ometime after the yellow sun had completed its arc and sunken once again into the coast they sailed over the Lucius Kellam Tunnel at the mouth of the Chesapeake Bay and out into the Atlantic Ocean. The blackened sea, sparkling in the moonlight, became one with the starry night sky. Only the faint glow of civilization to the west kept them company. The hull sliced seamlessly through the waves as a consistent wind drew them southward. Little had been spoken between Grey and Misty throughout the day, both of them pining for answers that neither could, or perhaps would, provide. Silence was indeed less agonizing than speaking any more questions. Grey watched as Misty gazed toward the coast, the locks of her long hair waving gently in the breeze, tracking behind her like the wake behind their vessel.

"I love you," he spoke at long last.

She turned toward him and smiled for just a moment, then turned away again. Grey was not offended by her silence. He understood her apprehensions about what their future may hold, and perhaps even about him as a man, in the face of this sudden and drastic change in the direction of their life together. The offering of those three words was one of reassurance that came without an expectation of reciprocation this time. He wished that he could tell her that everything would be alright, that McGuinness and Richter would soon turn up evidence that would exonerate him, but he was no more certain of these things than Misty. And so he offered only those three words.

They had made excellent time from Annapolis to the Atlantic, but the day had been long and in the darkness of the night both Grey and Misty were exhausted. Just past the lights of Virginia Beach, in the shadow of False Cape

State Park at the north end of the Outer Banks, they lowered the sails and dropped anchor.

"You should call your dad," said Misty as they stepped down into the cabin. "He said to call when we reached the Atlantic."

She walked the length of the cabin popping open the overhead butterfly hatches as Grey dialed Declan on the satellite phone.

"Dad, we're out of the Chesapeake."

"Good," said Declan. "Get some rest tonight, and keep a southern heading tomorrow. I want you to call me each night with an update on your coordinates."

"We got the money for Ankur. Are you going to tell us what's going on?"

"I'll tell you what you need to know when you need to know it. For now, all you need to do is trust me, alright?"

"OK. So what's our destination? That I need to know."

"Freeport."

"Bahamas?"

"Yes."

"Alright. I'll talk to you tomorrow."

Grey hung up and headed for bed where Misty was already tucked beneath the sheets. He lay down next to her, his chest pressed against her back, and wrapped his arms around her warm body, her steady breath rocking him gently with the ocean waves. She pushed her body into his and his embrace tightened.

"Where are we headed?" she whispered.

"The Bahamas."

"I guess if you have to run there are worse places."

He smiled and kissed the back of her head. A cool breeze drifted in through the open hatches, and the soothing aroma of the sea filled their new home.

"Grey?"

"Yes."

"I love you too."

Grey awoke the next morning to the warmth of the sun and a void in the bed where Misty had slept. He could hear her voice speaking to someone from the deck outside. A steaming mug of coffee awaited him on the galley countertop, which he collected before stepping up the ladder, prepared to scold her for making an unauthorized phone call. Instead he found her dripping wet, wrapped in a towel and leaning over the gunwale in conversation with a pair of burly sportsmen in a fishing boat.

"Morning!" said one fisherman when Grey appeared. "We were just admiring your beauty here. Her brightwork is flawless. What's she called?"

"Well thank you," he replied. "Her name will remain a secret though. This is her maiden voyage. I'm being gentle until I learn her rhythm."

The fishermen grinned and Misty turned away with a bashful snicker.

"Well enjoy her," said the fisherman. "She's a real charmer."

They tipped their hats and motored away as Misty stood to kiss Grey.

"Good morning, mi amor," she said with a smile.

"Good morning," he replied. "Did I miss something?"

"Well, I don't think they were talking about the boat."

"No?"

"Since I can't run, I thought I'd go for a morning swim."

"In this cold? The water must be freezing."

"It's not so bad, but I didn't think there would be anyone else out here."

"Yeah?"

Misty peered around to be sure that the other boat had gone, then looked back at Grey slyly as she let her towel fall to the deck.

"I see," he said, gazing at her beautiful, glistening naked body. "They were talking about *you*."

"Yep!" she chirped, raising her arms above her head and bouncing teasingly. She grabbed her hair into a ponytail and spun around, wringing the water out of it onto Grey's feet.

"You're chipper this morning," he laughed.

"I've decided that we might as well make the best of this situation."

"Agreed," he said.

"And I think it would be bad luck for us to sail this beautiful yacht any farther without giving her a proper naming ceremony."

"You don't think we should keep moving?"

"Nobody even knows we've left yet."

"OK. After breakfast?"

"OK!" said Misty, bouncing back down into the cabin to get dressed and prepare their first meal of the day. Within the fully stocked cold storage compartment she found two bottles of Dom Pérignon that Ankur had left for them specifically for christening the vessel. Given the circumstances it would be an unconventional christening, but then she was an unconventional vessel. Perhaps she deserved a ceremony as unique as her character.

Misty popped open one bottle of champagne and poured a mimosa for each of them to savor with breakfast while Grey drafted a minimalistic speech to celebrate the yacht's minimalistic design—a beautiful and elegant, yet natural and unpretentious flow of careful consideration. His words were brief but honest and heartfelt. When they had finished eating, they cleared the table and the galley of any untidiness and carefully wiped clean all surfaces that they had touched since departing. Two fresh glasses of champagne were poured, and Grey and Misty stepped cautiously to the bow in their bare feet, carrying with them the second unopened bottle of champagne.

"As tradition has demanded for thousands of years," Grey began, "sailors have called upon Poseidon, Neptune, god of the sea, and Boreas, Eurus, Zephyrus, and Notus, gods of the winds, to bless their vessels and deliver good fortune with the appellation of ships both new and renewed. And so now we call upon you, O God of the wind and the seas, and of all things that move and breathe, to bless this vessel as it carries us forth into a new chapter of our life. By your breath she will carry us upon your waters, and we ask for safe and swift passage on our journey, wherever it may lead.

"This vessel was designed and built with your gracious gifts, and likewise her name was selected to celebrate one of the most precious of those gifts. The name of my second love on this beautiful earth of yours is derived from that of my first."

He looked at Misty, smiling back at him, patiently awaiting the words that would follow.

"We hereby christen this vessel the *Mistical Reflection*, may she carry us from the clutches of evil and into the welcoming arms of justice."

Grey and Misty raised their glasses, and with a full swing she broke the bottle of champagne over the bow of the yacht. They took a celebratory drink, as did the sea, and they moved to the stern where Misty peeled away the seal revealing the radiant white designation against the rich wood tones of the hull.

The anchor was weighed and the sails raised, and they proceeded to sail southward as Declan had instructed.

A love for the sea had been instilled in Grey since early childhood. His father had earned his degree in engineering at the US Naval Academy before serving on a nuclear submarine during the Cold War, and although he had tolerated the months beneath the surface, on top of the water with the wind in his sails was where Declan had always seemed most contented. Grey's few memories of his mother before her untimely departure from this world were of her on the family's yacht alongside his father. It was a blessing, he thought, that the joyous memories had endured beyond those of hospital rooms. After her death, Grey had taken her place as his father's sailing partner, learning to travel by the wind and the sea years before he learned to drive a car. The joy of sailing, however, seemed to vacate Declan with the loss of his beloved wife, and the father-son voyages grew fewer until eventually they ceased entirely.

Grey recalled the multitude of awards and commendations displayed on a wall of the office in his childhood home. He had examined those colorful ribbons and medals with wide-eyed fascination, but from the perspective of a child with no understanding of their significance. It wasn't until he had grown that Grey realized his father was what many would call a hero, though Declan's humility would never betray any notion that he thought so highly of himself. Perhaps, Grey thought, that was precisely what made him a hero.

Few things brought Grey the fulfillment of knowing he had satisfied his father's silent pride. As far back as he could remember he had been trained by Declan in a broad range of military subjects, from martial arts to weapons, sailing to evasive driving, and although he had questioned their usefulness for a boy more interested in a civilian life, he had excelled at all of them. He had maintained perfect grades in school followed by an impressive career trajectory, and it devastated him that his immaculate record had been tarnished. He wondered how long it would be before his mistakes were forgiven, and if even then he could forgive himself. Recovering the integrity that he had spent a lifetime building would take a great deal of time and effort. Such a delicate thing—integrity—more so than he had realized. And what was perhaps even worse, he had compromised that of his father whom he had always idolized. God only knew what laws Declan was breaking to protect his only son. Fraud—for sure. Identity theft—perhaps. Bribery of a public officer. Obstruction of justice. Aiding and abetting a fugitive. The list went on, and the question of the money was an entirely separate issue that Grey could not even begin to explain. His family had always been comfortable, but wealthy, certainly not.

But Misty was right; there was no use dwelling on these things. After all, this was their maiden voyage upon the *Mistical Reflection.* Perhaps she could erase the mistakes of their past and they could start all over somewhere new, somewhere untainted by their sins and the sins of their adversaries. That was the beautiful thing about the sea—the possibilities were endless. The grain of the ancient wooden ship's wheel under his fingertips served as a reminder to Grey that a tarnished past did not need to dictate one's future. It gave him hope.

The yacht's cold storage and pantry had been well stocked, and with her speed there would be no need to make berth until they reached Freeport. Hurricane season seemed to have made a fortunately early retreat, and there was no significant weather on the radar. Grey was thankful for that at least. They hugged the coastline as closely as they could, hoping to avoid both the potential trap of the Intracoastal Waterway and the vicious winds of the Gulf Stream for as long as possible. Days on the ocean were taken slower than that first on the Chesapeake. The sunset over the Outer Banks set the night ablaze as they safely cleared the treacherous Diamond Shoals off Cape Hatteras, the sandy floor ever visible beneath its shallow waters. The cool autumn air of northern latitudes grew warmer with each day that stretched just a bit longer than the one before it. From behind the tide they watched it crash along the coast, its reds and yellows turning green once more. Skylines emerged and disappeared behind them.

Myrtle Beach

Charleston

Savannah

St. Augustine

A glacier blue sky and mirrored sea graced the days, but the nights were ever cloaked in dead quiet blackness leaving just that haunting glow from the distant coast and the subtle sounds of waves that would sustain long after all life had left the earth. It felt to both Grey and Misty as if they were completely alone in the world—a world that was entirely theirs, and yet not. They were king and queen of an immense, empty kingdom. Every evening they would call Declan, endure a brief exchange, and receive no new information from him, though it was clear he was up to something. Behind his voice they could hear the scenes change each night—busy city streets—flight announcements—elevator bells—silence.

"We're lucky," said Misty as she lay on the deck gazing up at the night sky.

"Yeah?"

"Like fugitive pirates," she smiled. "No rules."

"Except you didn't do anything wrong."

"Neither did you."

"I suppose."

"I wonder where we'll end up."

"Home," he replied, "I hope."

"Miss it already?"

"Don't you?"

She leaned over and kissed his cheek.

"Not yet," she said.

"I wish we hadn't dragged Ankur into this."

"We didn't have a choice."

"There's always a choice."

Just north of Fort Lauderdale they came about and headed east. The Florida horizon shrunk and disappeared behind the curve of the earth as the *Mistical Reflection* and her lovers sailed into the Gulf Stream. Its southeast current overcame the calm of the coastline, ruthlessly fighting against them with every crested wave and slowing their pace as if to steal away their advantage. Wall after deep blue wall beat against the hull and overtopped the gunwales as the yacht broke with equal ruthlessness through each one. The current, though, had been anticipated and would lead them northeast to their destination within the day. Even the power of the wind could not stop Grey and Misty as they learned to handle their still unfamiliar vessel and use that power to their advantage. The trio intuitively became as one.

Far off in open waters, they watched as a US Coast Guard Cutter approached a yacht on the same path. A Special Purpose Craft was dispatched to intercept the boat, which the crew of servicemen boarded for investigation. The Coast Guard, unlike the police, required no reasonable suspicion or probable cause to stop any vessel in their jurisdiction, and Grey had feared such an encounter from the outset. He was thankful for the other craft having lifted their burden. There was little doubt in his mind that his face and Misty's were now known to law enforcement from coast to coast. He took a breath as a gust of wind sent a chill down his spine.

Three short hours later the tropical reef of Grand Bahama came into view.

# 10

## Back in Annapolis

Ankur's shop became a lonely place with the departure of the *Mistical Reflection*. The vacant space she had left behind was bittersweet to the craftsman who hoped that her new owners were taking as much joy in sailing her as he had in building her. He left the door open to the sunrise over the harbor, its autumn breeze filling the dimly lit shop with that beloved fresh perfume as he lay on the couch to make up the sleep sacrificed for final preparation of the vessel the night before.

He was awakened later that afternoon by the creek of the shop's front door off the street as a pair of unwelcome, but not unexpected guests came through.

"We're looking for Ankur Patel," said one, extending his FBI credentials. Ankur stood, rubbing the sleep from his eyes.

"That's me. What's this about?"

"We'd like to talk to you about Grey Cavanaugh," said Richter. "He's a client of yours, is he not?"

"Sure."

"Can you tell us when you saw him last?"

"Not really. It's been a while."

"That's interesting," Richter challenged, "because we know he was here just two days ago."

Ankur eyed them both silently.

"Look, Mr. Patel," McGuinness broke in, "nobody's after you, but we need to know about your business with Mr. Cavanaugh."

"I built him a boat. What's to know?"

"May we see the boat?"

"No problem," replied Ankur without missing a beat. He led them out the back door to the dock. Nestled amongst the line of half-million dollar yachts tied to the pier, the afternoon sun bouncing from their fiberglass and aluminum and steel hulls, hid a humble, wooden thirty-foot daysailer. Ankur stepped onto the deck.

"Beautiful, isn't she? You guys sail?"

"This is it?" replied Richter, unimpressed. McGuinness cocked a slight grin and turned away to conceal it.

"This is it," Ankur confirmed proudly.

The young agent walked up and down the dock alongside the vessel, looking it over. His disappointment was evidenced by his scowl as he noted the lack of a cabin. There was no way this boat was built for Grey and Misty to flee.

"Not much to look at," he said.

"Perhaps to a layman," replied Ankur.

Richter scoffed.

"May we talk to your son?" McGuinness asked, struggling to flatten his smirk. "I understand he works with you."

"By all means," Ankur complied, stepping back onto the dock and heading into the shop. He listened closely to the agents speaking softly to one another as he walked away, but he could not hear a word of what they said.

Back inside he rousted Kiel from his sleep in the Eames Lounge in the back office. Startled, the young apprentice kicked over the flat beer that he had left on the desk in front of him that morning. *That's his German side*, his father thought, *and I love him for it.* After all, it was the boy's mother who had left them both with a love for fine craft beer, Ankur in his nostalgia and Kiel in his DNA. And in her love for the two of them, she had joyfully gifted her son with a name that celebrated both her own German heritage and the nautical legacy of Ankur's. They were her anchor and her keel, keeping her secure—balanced—safe. Now that she was gone they did the same for each other.

"The FBI is here about Grey," said Ankur as he grabbed a rag to wipe up the mess. "Remember what I told you."

The two of them walked back out to the dock where McGuinness and Richter stood waiting. Their still inaudible conversation ceased as they looked to the craftsmen and introduced themselves to Kiel.

"Your father was just showing us the boat you two built for Mr. Cavanaugh," said Richter.

"Beautiful, isn't she?"

"Sure. Did you notice anything strange about Grey the last time you saw him?"

"Strange? Not that I recall. He seems like a good guy."

"So you don't know him all that well."

"Not really. My father knows him better. I just work on the boats, you know. What do you think he did anyway?"

"We think he may be involved with some people. The details really don't involve you, but we're concerned about his safety."

From the corner of his eye, Ankur noticed McGuinness watching him closely, examining his expressions and movements as Richter questioned his son.

"Is this the first boat Mr. Cavanaugh has commissioned you for?" Richter continued to probe.

"Yes."

"I ask because we've been reviewing his finances, and we know what he paid you. Seems pretty steep for such a simple craft."

"You're obviously not a sailor," Kiel replied. "If you were you'd know this kind of craftsmanship and quality is expensive. Ask around; you'll have a hard time finding a client of ours who isn't pleased with every penny they spent."

"We'll do that," McGuinness interrupted before Richter could say any more. "Thank you for your cooperation. We'll be in touch."

Ankur led the agents back through his shop, watching as they studied every angle of the place on their way to the door—the vessels still unfinished, specialty lumber from all over the globe, motors and parts, the neatly arranged plans and walls of alphabetically organized books. McGuinness politely handed the craftsman his card and asked that he call if he heard anything from Grey. As they got into their rental car and drove away, a black Cadillac with tinted windows and Illinois plates pulled up to the curb across the street.

# 11

## The Suit

"Well, those guys were useless," said Richter, shaking his head as they drove up Main Street away from Ankur's shop. "At least we got his suit. Hopefully forensics can pull something useful from it. Too bad the bastard had it cleaned."

"Robert," McGuinness replied, "why would the guy have left his suit at the hotel for us to find if he had done this? You think he's just giving us evidence now?"

"Criminals make stupid mistakes."

"That's a big mistake. I'm telling you, we're wasting our time here."

"So you bought that Ankur guy's story?"

"Did you see another wooden boat around that was big enough for them to run away in?"

Richter thought for a moment.

"Maybe they're already gone."

McGuinness looked at him silently, then back at the road. Richter took out his phone and dialed the field office back in St. Louis.

"We need two surveillance teams on Grey Cavanaugh's home and office. I want to be notified of any activity immediately, and if they don't catch any movement by noon tomorrow I need to know that too. We're taking his suit to the DC forensics lab for analysis. Hopefully that'll give us enough evidence to pick him up—if we can find him by then. We'll stick around here until we hear from you."

The two agents stopped briefly at the Westin to collect their package before heading onto Highway Fifty west toward Washington.

# 12

## Freeport

"They found your suit."

Grey dropped his fork on the plate at the words his father spoke through the satellite phone.

"What's going on—" Misty tried to ask, but Grey cut her off, putting his finger to his lips and then covering his ear to block out the bustle of the busy Freeport bar. She turned and looked through the crowd beneath the canopy and across the beach.

"There were traces of Mancini's blood inside a sleeve," Declan went on, "and they know you've fled."

"Shit."

"This was expected. They still don't know where you are. The FBI paid Ankur a visit the day you left. Don't worry, he covered for you, but that will only slow them down. They're working things out. And there's one more thing."

"Great," said Grey, "I can't wait."

"The mob isn't far behind. They've had a car on Ankur's shop for days. Don't stress, I'm working on it, but

I wanted you to know. I've got an associate keeping an eye on you down there, but watch your surroundings."

"What?" Grey asked, looking around.

"Don't bother looking for him," said Declan. "You won't see him unless he wants you to. It's for your own safety."

Grey hung up and looked at Misty as she put her hands on the table and leaned forward.

"Well?"

"We're OK for now," he told her, "but we need to start paying attention. I want to move the boat tonight—just a few miles east, away from town. We'll anchor offshore."

Misty leaned back and looked toward the beach again, drawing shapes with her toes in the thin layer of sand on the floor. A cool breeze drifted through the palms surrounding the canopy. The soothing sound of their fronds brushing together unified with that of the gentle tide. The weather was mild outside, but within them both brewed an epic storm.

"It's so blue," she said.

Grey took a breath and smiled, gazing at the soft glow of Misty's skin in the afternoon Caribbean sun. Condensation dripped from the glass in front of her into small pools on the table, soaking into the wood grain through which she drew her fingertips, tracing lines like a map with no destination. A slight shiver resonated through her body, and goose bumps rose on her chest and arms. His eyes followed her long hair draped over her shoulder and scanned down her body, across the perfect curves behind her bikini top and down to her belly button where the edge of the table drew his gaze up again. She turned back to him and their eyes met, and she smiled.

"We're OK?" she asked.

"We're OK."

"Do we have to leave?"

"No."

"Good. I like it here."

"Me too."

He watched as she stood and walked from the table, her hips swaying with the slow, subtle darbuka beat of the Latin band beneath the canopy outside. Her bare feet landed silently on the worn wood planks of the floor with the lows of the Spanish guitar, and her toned shoulders shifted with hiss of the maracas. The colored lights above bounced from the perspiration shine of her still fair skin. She leaned over the bar, her knees alternately bending, rocking her back and forth. The bartender appeared before her immediately, bypassing the other thirsty patrons, stepped away for a moment, and returned with two shots. Misty took them and glided back to the table with the same graceful swagger, Grey having never taken his eyes off of her. She took her seat again and slid a glass across the table to him.

"But you don't like tequila," he said.

"I like the way it makes me feel."

They shot back the smooth Patrón and bit into their lime slices. Misty held her head back and her eyes closed, the colors of her flowing hair bright in the light of the setting sun. She tossed her head from side to side, then she held still letting the sun warm her face. Behind her Grey watched the *Mistical Reflection* anchored off the beach, rocking in the waves. A pelican had perched upon the bow, still and silently searching the water below for its next meal, its long, narrow beak almost parallel with the mast. It curved its neck and put its beak beneath its wing for a moment, cleaning the underside of its feathers, then adjusted again to the position of the watchman. A moment later it spread its wings and lifted off, gliding gracefully across the horizon just above the surface of the water. Abruptly, it swooped up into the sky and then dove back down and splashed into the waves and floated, tossing its catch back into its swollen beak.

The Spanish guitar played on, its groovy flamenco derivation drawing ever-bolder movement from those souls too reserved to move in such a way in the daylight. As the sky darkened, the beach itself became an extension of the dance floor, glowing orange with the flickering of tiki torches and fires in the sand. The night was warm despite the breeze and the line of heavy, low clouds rolling in from the south. Lightning feathered silently across the sky in the distance, but the people on the beach danced on. Grey and Misty watched them from their table between her trips to the bar, and then he would watch her, knowing he was not the only one.

He took her hand without a word and led her from the table and out into the night, their bare feet slipping inconspicuously between the dozens of others shuffling in the sand. Neither were dancers, nor had they ever danced together in the company of others, but theirs was a journey of firsts. They danced closely, the strands of her hair weaving through the stubble of his beard. They felt the warm breath of one another on their necks, growing ever warmer and more rapid as they moved together. Grey watched the other travelers and locals swaying about them with that same intimate symmetry, and he wondered about the secrets hidden within each of them. He closed his eyes.

"Hold me tighter," said Misty. "I'm a little drunk."

He pulled her to him, his fingertips following the strings of her bikini around to her back. He felt raindrops on the back of his hand.

"I've got you," he said. "I won't let you fall."

"And I won't let you."

"We could stay out here all night."

"It's starting to rain," she said.

"That's OK."

The rain fell harder, and with the lightning came claps of thunder. The tiki flames fizzled out, but the fires in the sand hissed and blazed on. Clouds blocked the glow of the moon, hiding the horizon so the night sky seemed to begin where the tide crashed onto the beach and end nowhere. The other dancers moved from the wet sand and back beneath the canopy, but Grey and Misty stayed, still dancing as they had been, but alone with the rain and the fire and the night.

"Maybe it can always be this way," she said.

"I guess we'll see."

"Just you and me. You and me against the world."

"Not the world," he said. "Just a few."

"They can't chase us forever."

"I think they will. Until they catch us."

"But they won't."

"What?"

"Catch us."

"No," he said. "They won't."

"You think we could hear the music from the boat?"

"Maybe."

She took his hand and they walked into the cold black surf toward the *Mistical Reflection*, her lights casting streams of color across the waves. When they were waist deep he stopped her and looked back toward the beach and the wooden shanty bar canopy beyond. There Grey caught a fleeting glimpse of a man with skin as dark as the night who seemed to watch them for a moment and then disappear into the mass of drinkers and dancers, none of whom seemed to have noticed Grey and Misty's departure, if they had ever noticed their presence at all.

"Come on," she said. "It's not that far of a swim."

"Did you notice anyone watching us?"

"Nobody can see us out here."

"We can barely see each other."

"I know," she whispered, her voice subdued by the sound of the rain on the water's surface. "So you'll have to hold onto me tight."

"We'll move the boat tomorrow. Too dangerous tonight."

"OK."

They turned back toward the boat and walked until they could no longer feel the sand beneath their feet, then they swam, each using one hand to paddle and the other never releasing the grasp between them. When they reached the *Mistical Reflection* they climbed aboard at the rope ladder over the gunwale then pulled it up and went below to the cabin. Grey opened a bottle of rum and lit candles and they drank, listening to the faint sounds of the music from the shore and the thunder, watching the lightning flash eerily across each other's face.

In the morning the sea was calm and the sun beamed through the portholes. They opened the butterfly hatches to vent the humidity from inside and bathed in the ocean before sitting down to breakfast on the deck. The bar on the beach was empty and quiet. A few vacationers were out for a morning walk in the surf. Shirtless fishermen stood in the rich turquoise shallows, casting and reeling and casting and reeling. Others cleaned bright green mahi-mahi and Atlantic blue marlin on the pier. Seagulls wailed overhead and roamed the beach, scavenging for scraps left the night before. The storm had all but vanished in the northern sky, and the south was clear.

"I saw a fish market in town," said Grey. "I'll go in this morning and pick up a few things before we move east. And I'll get some hair dye for you. We need to change the way we look."

"What color?"

"I'll get something you'll like."

"You should stop shaving," she said, running her fingers down his cheek.

"Yeah. And you can cut my hair when I get back."

"You don't want me to come?"

"You can stay here if you want. Work on that tan."

He untied his kayak and tossed it over the side and climbed in.

"Don't leave without me," he said.

"I'll be waiting."

She watched as he paddled off and the tide carried him to shore. He pulled the kayak up on the beach and left it there, walking beneath the canopy of the vacant bar toward the street and disappearing.

She was alone for the first time on the *Mistical Reflection*. It was a foreign feeling, but not an entirely unwelcome one. She was alone and yet she felt safe, even with the knowledge of the fate that sought her. She cut up a lime and mashed some mint leaves and brought the bottle of Caribbean rum that they had uncorked the night before up to the deck and laid out with a book, but she never opened it. The boat rocked gently in the calm waters with a slow spin that gave her an ever-changing panoramic view of the sparkling blue sea and the flat green island. A dorsal fin emerged from the surf, then another, bearing toward the beach. Two bottlenose dolphins darted in with the tide and thrashed in alternating rhythm where it met the sand, entrapping and stunning small fish to make a meal of them.

She took a sip of her mojito and rolled over, dangling her arm over the side, her fingers dipping into the water as the boat rocked. An angelfish nibbled on her fingertips. She snickered and closed her eyes. If the chase would take her to paradise, she didn't so much mind it. Perhaps even the end was not worth fearing if it would end in a place like this. Nothing could be more poetic than she and Grey dying young together on the sea, their love never having the chance to dilute with time and separation.

She rolled onto her back again and rested her head on the coiled nylon anchor rode and held the cold glass of rum on her skin between her breasts. She took in a deep breath and sighed. The ice in the glass vibrated and clinked with the steady beating of her heart. Through the cloudy cocktail the sun's rays cast a white glow over the obscured blue horizon, and she yearned for nothing at all.

Grey returned some hours later, paddling back out to her with a crate of groceries balanced and cabled to the kayak behind his seat. They pulled the kayak aboard and stocked the cold storage compartment, then they weighed anchor and raised the sails and moved east to anchor again in deeper waters off an unsettled beach.

Weeks of bliss passed by, soured only slightly by the brief and mysterious evening calls with Declan that seemed the same each night. Every two or three days they sailed short distances down the coastline to anchor again in a new spot off a new beach in hopes of avoiding unwanted attention.

They spoke little of the circumstances that had led them to this place, and although they mused within, those circumstances remained as mysterious as they had been on the day that Agents McGuinness and Richter had come into their lives.

Musing had led Misty to one nagging suspicion. How and why she still had not worked out, but the Star Silo project was somehow the root of all of it. They sailed past the High Rock Lighthouse on the southern coast of Grand Bahama, its candy-striped tower standing tall above the surf. Grey lowered the sails and tossed the anchor over the gunwale.

"I read about that lighthouse," said Misty.

"Yeah?"

"It's supposed to guide 'lost and drifting souls,' according to the reverend who built it."

"What's it telling you?"

She laughed and looked across the water and up toward the rocks. "Why do you think they didn't want us talking?" she asked.

"Who?"

"On the project. Is that normal? I've never worked on a commercial development that size before."

"Neither have I," he said.

"Why do you think they chose you?"

"I don't know."

"You don't find it peculiar?"

"I don't know."

Some days they swam or paddled to shore to run the beach and remember the feel of the ground beneath their feet. They built sandcastles at low tide and watched them disappear back into the ocean as if they had never been. Some days they saw people. Others not. Cruise ships came and left Freeport harbor in the distance. Sailboats and fishing vessels passed on the horizon. They spoke some and read and made love often and drank more. When the sun grew hot they took shelter in the shade of the great white sails, and as their stock of food and drink and books ran low, they came about and headed west again toward Freeport.

They anchored off the familiar beach with the open-air bar and paddled in, tying their kayaks to a palm tree. A calypso band was setting up steel drums where the flamenco guitarist had sat before. They walked past beneath the canopy and the Bahamian flag and hanging fishnets and colorful glass globes on ropes.

"What day is it?" Grey asked.

"Does it matter?"

They boarded a bus and rode through the streets of Freeport and its roundabouts to Port Lucaya Marketplace. Bright pastel pink and green and yellow buildings of stucco and wood with metal roofs housed shops and restaurants that left doors open to invite in tourists. Local artisans displayed their make in rows of tiny booths packed with colorful clothing and woodcarvings and novelty shot glasses. Palm trees grew sparsely from the brick pathways and provided little shade. Pink and white hibiscus grew from the gardens throughout.

They shopped for a while and then followed a shaded path beneath overhanging palm fronds along the water's edge around a small peninsula in the marina to a secluded spot and sat on the edge with their feet dangling over the water. Misty looked at the lighthouse across the way.

"I've been wondering something," she said.

"What's that?"

"What were those hidden rooms and secret passageways for?"

"Where?"

"In the building plans. The Star Silo."

He looked up and squinted, then looked at her. "There were no hidden rooms or secret passageways," he said.

"Sure there were. I designed bookcases to conceal them. It was beautiful, actually."

"Misty, there was nothing like that in the plans I drew."

"They were interior rooms on the top two floors adjacent to the elevator shaft."

"No, there was the floor lobby, and then office space," he said. "No secret rooms."

"Are you saying someone altered the plans?"

"I'm saying I don't know what you saw. Maybe you misread them."

"Don't condescend. I know how to read plans as well as you do."

"Well, I don't know what you saw."

She looked across the water again toward the lighthouse.

"Maybe that's why they didn't want us talking."

"I want a change of scenery," he said. "We've been hanging around this island long enough."

"Where do you want to go?"

"Nassau's close."

"We should talk to your dad first."

"No. We don't need his permission. Do you want to go?"

She smiled at him.

"Yes."

# 13

## The Sommer House

The lawns and rooftops of South St. Louis were white with snow, ribbons of smoke rising out of chimneys and disappearing into the gray sky. The streets were quiet. Agent Richter flipped through the radio stations as he and McGuinness drove toward Misty's parents' home.

"You know what bothers me," he said.

"What's that?"

"Cavanaugh's father. I looked into him more. He was a military guy before he was an engineer; he respects authority. Why won't he talk to us?"

"Probably because we're looking at his son for murder."

"I guess."

"Besides," said McGuinness, "if they told him anything about where they were going then they told her parents too, and we're more likely to get something out of them anyway. Their daughter isn't being accused of anything."

They parked on the street in front of the old brick house and walked across the yard to the front door and knocked.

"Who is it?" yelled a voice from the other side.

"FBI, Mr. Sommer. We have a few questions about your daughter and Grey Cavanaugh."

The door cracked open slightly.

"Identification," he said.

Both agents pulled out their credentials, and Tom Sommer took a long look at each before allowing them through the door and closing it behind them.

"Forgive me," he said. "Some reporters have been showing up unannounced since our daughter left with Grey, asking us questions about organized crime and all that nonsense. We have neighbors, you know. There's just no decency. I guess we have you to thank for that."

"I'm sorry about that, Mr. Sommer," said McGuinness. "But nobody has called Grey Cavanaugh a suspect."

"Person of interest, suspect, it's all the same. I'm not an idiot, but you guys must be pretty dense if you think Grey killed anybody. Young men don't get any more honest."

"Then help us out," said Richter. "Where are they?"

"Ha!" Tom Sommer belted, turning toward the next room. "Virginia, where's Misty?"

Misty's mother came through the doorway with a steaming mug in her hand. "On vacation, Tom. Don't be rude. Invite our guests in for some coffee. It's cold out there."

"Guests," he scoffed, watching the agents follow his wife into the living room and take seats on his couch. He sat down in his armchair across from them and glared.

"Mrs. Sommer," said McGuinness, "we're not after your daughter. We just want to talk to Grey Cavanaugh. Do you know where they went?"

"Vacation," she said, pouring a mug for each of them. "I told you."

"Right. Do you know where they went on vacation?"

She shrugged. "Where does anyone go on vacation?"

The two agents looked at each other, then at Tom who sat quietly smirking.

"Did they say when they would be back?"

"No," she smiled.

"Did Misty give you a phone number? Any way to reach her?"

"I guess she took her cell phone with her."

"No. It's still at their house."

"Oh," said Virginia. "Then I guess she forgot it."

"Most people don't forget their cell phones when they go out of town," said Richter. "Unless they don't want to be found."

"Do you want to be found on vacation?"

"Kind of an odd time for a vacation, don't you think?"

"No."

"No?"

"Lots of people take vacation from the winter," she said.

"Not when they're under investigation by the FBI."

She smiled again. "How's your coffee? Do you need sugar?"

"No, thank you," said McGuinness. "Mrs. Sommer, we don't want to hurt Misty or Grey. We just want to talk to them and figure out what happened in Chicago. Is there anything at all you can tell us?"

"Oh, sure," she said. "I'll tell you a story about Misty. When she was a little girl—not even five years old yet—she insisted on learning to ride a bike. So we got her a little one speed with coaster brakes and training wheels and a bell and pink tassels on the handlebars, you know. She loved that bike. She would spend all day riding all over the neighborhood. After about a week or so she realized that the training wheels were slowing her down—she couldn't take corners as fast as she wanted to. So, without telling us, she got into her daddy's toolbox and found a wrench and took those training wheels right off. Then she took her bike out all alone early in the morning and taught herself to ride without them."

"So she was a strong-willed girl," said McGuinness.

"But that's not the end. When she started school we let her ride her bike there, then to her little friends' houses. Sometimes she would leave in the morning and we wouldn't see her until after sunset. Other parents said we shouldn't give such a young girl that kind of freedom. They said it was dangerous, but Tom and I always believed that children need some independence. That's how we were raised. If you trap them at home and set all sorts of rules and tell them everything they should and shouldn't do, they never learn anything on their own, and they grow up afraid of the world.

"Well, by high school Misty had a bigger, faster bike. She was competing in races and beating everyone. Then one day she was in an accident. She was passing another biker—a close friend—who cut her off trying to keep the lead and they both went down. But instead of blaming her friend, Misty ran to her, lifted her from the road, and pulled her out of the way so she wouldn't be hit by the other bikers. That girl barely had a scratch, but Misty had gone down hard. We took her for X-rays, and her forearm was broken all the way through."

Richter leaned back on the couch and looked at the fire burning in the fireplace. He took a sip of his coffee.

"Now," Virginia went on, "of course she couldn't ride her bike very well with a broken arm. No more competing—not for a while anyway. She had been hoping for a cycling scholarship, but her injury had set her back behind her peers. Most people would be discouraged, right? Not Misty. Instead she just took up running, and she hasn't stopped since.

"So, you see, you can't stop her. You can put obstacles in her way, but she'll find a way around them. You can chase her, but you're not likely to catch her. And God forbid you put someone she loves in danger—someone like Grey—she'll put herself in the line of fire before she'll watch them fall. And I believe he would do the same for her."

# 14

## Could You Be Loved

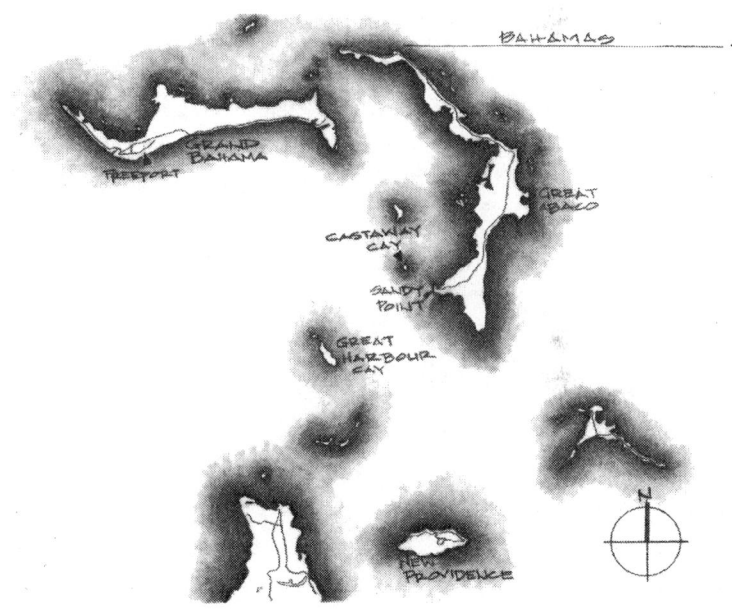

**W**ind whipped across the jib and the mainsail as the *Mistical Reflection* cruised south, cutting through the surface of the deep blue Caribbean water. Broken waves spilled over the gunwales and shadows swept across the deck as they heeled and tacked in the changing winds, the salty spray leaving the sea streaming over the sails glowing radiant white, backlit by the sun. They followed the reef that stretched from the east end of Grand Bahama to Sandy Point on the south of Great Abaco. Misty lounged on a seat beside Grey at the helm, watching the island shrink behind them. She brushed her hair out of her face and looked up at him.

"How do you stay happy?" she asked.

"Me?"

"In general."

"Are you happy?"

"I'm a lot of things, but yes, for now."

"Ready about!" said Grey as he spun the wheel to turn the boat into the wind. The jib luffed and he released the starboard jib sheet as Misty trimmed the port and winched it taut. He looked at her and smiled, then back ahead with his hands on the wheel.

"Freedom," he said.

"Freedom?"

"Freedom is happiness. Know that you have a choice in everything you do. Never feel trapped. Always be free."

The wind began to steady and ease their course south as Bob Marley sang "Could You Be Loved" through the boat speakers. Misty hung her arm over the water and watched the reef and its shallows passing along the port side where the depth dropped leaving a defined line between bright turquoise and deep blue. A foamy wake trailed behind them and faded into the distance where it disappeared into the waves leaving no trace of where they had been. Far off boats appeared as specks on the horizon, but nowhere in any direction could they see another person, nor could they be seen as anything other than one of those specks on the horizon.

Misty stood and wrapped her hair in a messy bun, its dark amber shine distinguished against the sea blues like the natural wood tones of the *Mistical Reflection*. Grey watched her as she slowly headed toward the cabin, glancing over her shoulder at him just before she went below. Minutes later she appeared again with a piña colada in each hand and set one beside Grey. She moved behind him and put her hands on his shoulders and slid them down his arms and rested them on the backs of his hands, weaving her fingers between his wrapped around the wheel. She pushed up onto her toes and rested her chin on his shoulder and burrowed into his neck. He turned his head toward her and she kissed his cheek. He took a hand off the wheel and turned to face her and she kissed him deeply for a moment, then she stepped back and gazed into his eyes and he gazed back into hers.

"Should we stop?" he asked.

"No," she said. "Keep going."

She stepped away and released his hand to collect her drink and he watched her feet as they fell softly on the deck with each step drawing his gaze toward the bow. She traced the blackwood gunwale past the mainsail and she leaned against the mast and took a sip from her glass. The muscles of her back sent shadows crawling across her tanning skin. She shed her crop knit cover-up and tossed it back to the helm and the wind caught it and it fell at his toes.

"Ready about!" he called, spinning the wheel and releasing the port jib sheet. She swung away gracefully to avoid the jib as Grey cranked in the starboard sheet and the mainsail boom swept across the deck over the butterfly hatches. Misty stepped to the port side of the sailboat and eyed him around the mast for only a moment before looking ahead toward the bow. Then she made her way again. Each step landed on the decking with her perfectly soft touch—the ball of her foot, then her toes, then her heel.

He took a sip as he watched her ethereal sway, right to left, starboard to port, until she reached the compass inlay at the bow that matched the one just before his own feet. Loose strands of her hair blew behind her in the wind. She glanced back at him again, then ahead toward the open sea. She brushed the hair from her face and reached around to her back, pulling the strings loose from the bow of her bikini top and lifting it over her head. The thin fabric blew in the wind, and she tied it to the copper cleat on the gunwale beside her. From nearly fifty feet behind her Grey could see the narrow tan line across her back that showed the color her skin had been. The fair color of her innocence darkened just a little with each day spent in mystery. She slipped her fingers into the sides of her bikini bottom and slowly slid it off, bending at the waist, shimmying it down her toned legs, stepping out of it and shedding her last bit of clothing revealing that same abrupt opposition of color in her most intimate of places. She stood for a moment to let him admire her bare hourglass figure, then she knelt and lay on her back, hooking her bikini bottom to the cleat and sprawling in the sun on the deck with her arms above her head pointed to the stern in full exposure to the world that could not see her.

Grey's eyes scanned the vast blue horizon to the west and protruding green fragments of the reef to the east and fell once again to the icon of perfection at the bow framed by the glowing white sails. He left the helm and made his way forward to Misty against the resistance of the wind in his open shirt. When he reached her, he knelt above her head between her arms and placed his hands onto hers. The sun hit her body in a way he had never seen before. Blonde peach fuzz lent a golden shine to her bronze lines and curves. Tiny beads of perspiration sparkled on her chest in the pattern of her pores, perfectly untouched, rising and falling with her steady breath. Her eyes remained closed. He ran his hands down the length of her arms and bent over her and kissed her lips, the sweet taste of piña colada still on her tongue. When they released she sat up and turned toward him and looked into his eyes.

"I love you," she said.

"I love you."

She leaned back with her head to the bow and he knelt beside her. His fingertips caressed her cheek and traced her neck, her collarbone, leaving trails in the sweat across her breasts, down her abdomen to the goose bumps that had formed on her thighs. She gasped at his touch, her breath growing rapid. Neither flinched when the hull struck a wave and sent a cold spray across them. Saltwater dripped from the gunwales and from the jib onto the deck and from Grey's skin onto Misty's.

    She slipped her hands into his shirt and around his back and pulled him close as he breathed in the fragrance of tea tree and lavender in her hair. Her body rose and fell beneath him, her warm breath on his neck, her heartbeat resonating through his chest, and he saw behind her beautiful face painted in ecstasy the onyx and copper compass like a halo of endless possibilities. Wherever they were destined to be, they were destined to be together. He put his lips to hers and kissed her deeply as her embrace tightened around him and her back arched, and then they lay on the deck tangled together in the saltwater spray and the warm sun.

Night had fallen before they passed by Castaway Cay glowing in the east. Fireworks exploded over a cruise ship, each flash coming seconds before the sound reached them. Grey and Misty watched as they sailed by, imagining the raucous celebration of joyous children with their doting parents vacationing just a few miles away and unwise to the fugitives watching the same display from their quiet asylum. Misty shivered in the cool night wind and wrapped herself in a blanket. As the fireworks faded and disappeared, she lay on a seat at the helm and closed her eyes. Grey, though, could not sleep. They sailed past Great Harbour Cay to the west appearing only as a shadow in the night. Lights from other vessels emerged on the black horizon and disappeared again, but one to the north remained, maintaining the same distance and course through the hours of darkness between sunset and sunrise. Grey watched the light from the helm throughout the night as Misty slept peacefully wrapped in her blanket on the seat beside him.

As the sun began to rise the tiny light faded until it vanished entirely. Misty awoke and stretched beneath her blanket and lay there watching Grey at the helm, still wide-awake as if sleep were too audacious a notion to entertain even after nearly twenty-four hours under sail.

"We're getting close," he said. "There are more boats up ahead."

"How long was I sleeping?"

"Just a few hours. The wind abated overnight. We're down to about four knots. We have a few hours more before Nassau. You can go back to sleep if you want."

"It's OK. I want to see the island when we come in."

"OK."

"Aren't you tired?" she asked.

"I'm fine."

She watched him at the helm, his hands on the ancient wheel with a delicate passion that he reserved for only her and her reflection. His touch was gentle, and yet so strong, and she felt safe under his protection—safe enough to sleep, vulnerable on open waters. She knew that he would give his life to save hers without a moment's hesitation, and perhaps this was what scared her the most, because she also knew that she would do the same for him. Although they were not yet legally married, she felt that their spirits had become one long ago, and the eyes of God were infinitely more important than those of the law.

"There it is," said Grey as the Royal Towers of Atlantis rose ahead on the horizon. "Paradise Island."

Misty dropped the blanket onto the deck and leaned over the gunwale for a better view around the sails. The massive hotel complex that sprawled across Paradise Island with its pink towers dwarfed every other building on the skyline of the city of Nassau behind it.

"It's synthetic," she said. "But tasteful."

"Yes," Grey laughed. "I feel like I shouldn't, but I like it. The Lost City."

A cigar boat approached and went tearing by, polluting the serenity with its noise and speed and the stench of burning fuel. Grey cringed as he watched it shrink behind them and its broken wake crashed over the gunwales and onto the deck of the *Mistical Reflection*.

"That," he said, "is not freedom."

"No?"

"No more than an overpriced sports car. How far can they get on a tank of gas before they have to refuel? And what happens if they break down in open waters? It's pretend—a taste of freedom. Like a spoonful of ice cream when you wish you had a bowl." He ran his fingers across grain of the ship's wheel. "This is freedom."

They anchored off Colonial Beach on the west end of Paradise Island and bathed in the ocean before swimming to shore.

# 15

## Revelations

Tourists were just beginning to wake up and make their way to the resort beaches of Paradise Island to the east, but Grey and Misty's beach was empty. They let the rich blue tide carry them ashore, then they walked barefoot toward Atlantis with the waves rolling over their feet and pulling the white sand out from beneath them. Misty's sandals swung in her hand as a cruise ship coasted by into Nassau Harbour between Paradise Island and the city. They walked into the water and swam past the partitions and rocks separating private resorts on the west end of the island accessible only by boat, and then they continued east along Paradise Beach and cut through the *Casuarina* forest on a hidden sand trail that led onto a back road where nobody noticed them. Shop doors stood open in the colorful and quaint resort village outside of Atlantis along the southern line of Paradise Island. They turned away as they passed a patrolling officer of the Royal Bahamas Police in his white shirt and pith helmet and radio in his hand, but he paid them no mind.

Boats drifted in the harbor beneath the bridge as Grey and Misty crossed into Nassau. Tourists flocked in the streets, pouring off of cruise ships, studying maps and pointing in various directions, buying conch shells from peddlers at the water's edge. Picketers circled on the plaza in front of the Government House, passing beneath the shadow of its coral-colored Georgian Colonial façade. Christmas lights hung dimly twinkling in the daylight from palm trees and storefronts and private residences.

"I forgot it was winter," said Misty.

"Yeah."

"I miss the snow."

Grey took her hand and pulled her close as they walked. "We'll see it again," he said.

"Promise?"

"Of course. Christmas will just be a little different away from home, but we'll still spend it together."

"That's all we need," she said and kissed his cheek. "Each other."

"Yes. And I like this town."

"So colorful."

They stopped to eat at a restaurant downtown and sat on a curbside patio watching the streets crawl with life. Police officers in white gloves directed traffic, stopping cars at intersections to let pedestrians cross and then waving them through again.

"Do you think they know our faces down here?" she asked.

"If they do, I don't think they're looking. Nobody knows where we are."

"We hope."

"You think they do?"

"I think the more time that passes the worse our odds get," she said. "It's been over six weeks since we left, and like you said, they'll never stop looking for us. Until they catch us."

The waitress came to take their order and neither looked at her as they spoke. Grey's eyes followed her as she walked back inside where no lights burned and fans spun slowly over an empty room. She returned with their meal some time later and they had not spoken a word in between.

"We didn't call my dad last night," he said.

"You didn't want to."

"No."

"You think he's worried?"

"No. I think he knows things that we don't."

"How?"

"I don't know."

They ate their meal and paid with Stephen Johnson's credit card that Declan had given them and walked the streets of Nassau until the sun began to set. The Christmas lights twinkled brighter as the sky darkened. They crossed the bridge back to Paradise Island with the radiance of Atlantis fighting against the coming night, then they slipped from the back service road into the foliage and the sand trail and back onto the beach where there were no lights and walked in the sand until the rocks blocked their way. They swam around the rocks again using the distant lighthouse as their guide and fought the tide breaking on Colonial Beach until they reached the *Mistical Reflection* and climbed aboard.

Grey sat at the desk in the cabin staring at the satellite phone as Misty lay on the couch gazing into the orange glow of the sconces along the bulkheads. The yacht rocked in the waves. He picked up the phone and began to dial then set it down on the desk again and went to the galley and poured himself a drink.

"Do you want one?" he asked.

"No."

He sat beside her and drank the rum from his glass and chewed the ice until the glass was dry. The cabin was quiet save for the faint sound of the Bahamian surf, beautiful and perfect in its infinite rhythm. With closed eyes it could have been night or day.

The satphone rang, startling them both. Grey went to the desk and put it to his ear.

"You were supposed to call me," said Declan. "Every night."

"I know."

"Where are you?"

"Freeport. Where are you?" Grey heard the sound of an elevated train.

"You're not in Freeport. You're in Nassau."

"How do you know that?"

"Lies are dangerous, son. Especially now."

"Then stop it."

"I haven't lied to you."

"You haven't told me the truth."

"The time isn't right."

"Well, I'm not waiting any longer."

Declan sighed. "OK," he said. "Tomorrow."

"Tomorrow?"

"Tomorrow you'll go back into town. Wait at the foot of the Queen's Staircase at noon. A man will ask you for a light for his cigar. Give him a light and follow him. He'll tell you what you need to know."

Grey and Misty slept lightly, both waking frequently and pacing the cabin just to move and then lying down again. When the morning light began to break through the portholes they rose and dressed and left for the city, drying from the swim as they walked the empty beach and crossed the bridge and wandered the streets to pass the time. Within the jungle corridor of the Queen's Staircase the air was cool and quiet and still. Water cascaded down the vertical end wall, its vivid orange stone turning green with algae and moss. Misty shivered in the spray.

"What time is it?" she asked.

"Eleven fifteen."

Palms towered around and above them along the immense stone walls that let in little sunlight. A local woman sat near the entrance selling colorful hand-woven straw baskets and hats to tourists. Minutes passed slowly.

Their empty stomachs growled, but their nerves stifled the hunger. They sat on a stone, looking up the staircase, waiting.

At exactly noon a shadow was cast over them from behind.

"Excuse me," came a deep voice in a Bahamian accent. "Would you happen to have a light?"

Grey turned and looked up to the massive figure looming above, immediately recognizing the face that he had seen only once weeks before. The man held an unlit cigar in his night-black hand. Grey pulled a lighter from his pocket and handed it to the man who lit his cigar and turned away without speaking another word and walked toward the mouth of the corridor. They stood and followed him.

When he reached the street the man stopped at the passenger side of an old gray Jeep with no doors and motioned for them to get in. Misty sat close behind Grey. The man stepped into the driver's seat and started the engine with a roar and pulled onto the road.

"Where are we going?" asked Grey.

The man puffed on his cigar. "We are just driving," he said. "My name is Tobias. I am an associate of your father."

He extended his hand palm up over the shifter and Grey hesitantly shook it. He thought his knuckles would be crushed under Tobias's grip, that muscular arm covered in blurred scripts that could have been tattoos or scars.

"Your father and I have worked together for some years," he went on.

"I didn't know he had ever done work in the Bahamas."

"There is quite a lot you don't know about Declan, as I'm sure you've figured out."

"Yes."

"We have worked in many places. Sierra Leone. South Africa. Somalia. Various countries in the Middle East."

"So you're an engineer?"

"I have been many things. Retired now, officially, back in my home country. But people like your father and I are never really retired."

"What do you mean by that?"

Tobias took another puff as the wind whipped through the Jeep and left his smoke swirling in the air behind them. Misty sat quietly listening.

"I think you know what I mean," said Tobias.

"I have suspicions," Grey replied. "Tell me. Who do you work for?"

"I have been paid by crime syndicates. Drug cartels. Terrorist organizations. A number of foreign governments."

"And my father?"

"For longer than you've been alive, Declan has been a clandestine operative for a certain US government agency."

Grey looked at the road ahead silently. A gold crucifix swung from the rear view mirror.

"So you've been watching us?"

"Yes."

"And what happens next?" Misty jumped in. "We just sail around the Caribbean forever?"

"No," said Tobias. "You would be caught eventually. The FBI and the mob are much better at this than you are, and you've got both after you."

"Then what are we doing?"

"We're waiting."

"For what?"

"The word from Declan."

He pulled the Jeep over to the side of the road in downtown Nassau. The crucifix circled above the dashboard.

"That's all I can say for now. Just stay low, keep doing what you're doing. Hopefully you won't have to see me again, but I'll be watching. Be careful."

Grey and Misty climbed out of the Jeep and Tobias drove off leaving a trail of cigar smoke behind. They stood on the side of the road looking at each other, speechless. That night they called Declan, and the conversation was no different than they had been for weeks. Brief. Lacking information. Not a word was spoken of the meeting with Tobias, nor did Grey and Misty speak of it alone.

The weather cooled only slightly as the days passed, still reaching seventy degrees most afternoons. They sailed the full perimeter of New Providence and Paradise Island, walking the beaches, some busy with tourists, some with local fishermen, others entirely empty of any footprints but their own. The flat geography of the cays made them look even smaller than they were. If it weren't for the trees they could have seen straight from one end of the island to the sea on the other side. They spoke less, a vacant air left where words of Grey's family secrets so desperately sought release but remained trapped behind a pretense of honesty that neither was prepared to break down.

Christmas was spent quietly on the *Mistical Reflection*, just the two of them in the Caribbean sun. They swam in the morning and celebrated with a bountiful meal. Misty carved a pineapple in the shape of a Christmas tree and decorated it with berries and slices of kiwi and they sat close and picked at it and fed it to one another, laughing together. She snuck away from Grey with the cell phone to make a brief call to her parents though she knew she should not. They swam again in the afternoon and watched the sunset paint the sky and the ocean orange and indigo.

On New Years Eve they went to Atlantis and wandered the lavish casino and the expansive resort grounds designed and built from whimsical and fantastic dreams. Among massive columns and flowing archways water spilled perpetually from the mouths of sculpted sea creatures as others living swam in pools and rivers alongside stone terraces and under bridges. A giant manta ray glided silently like a shadow beneath the surface. A school of sharks circled in the shallows. A cavern doorway led to an underground aquarium where all the sea life visible from above and more could be seen from a dark and damp maze below. Faux ruins framed glass walls within the aquarium catacombs, offering a glimpse into the beautiful and terrifying world above which Grey and Misty had made their home. They stood peering into that world in awe, the pair silhouetted by the sunbeams in the blue glow before them. He took her hand in his and held it tightly.

They followed the path back out into the palms and the sun and by the pool and all of its swimming tourists below the bridge suite that connected the Royal Towers at the seventeenth floor. Misty looked up and raised her hand to shade her eyes from the sun.

"You know that's the most expensive hotel suite in the world?" she said. "Twenty-five thousand dollars a night."

Grey laughed.

"Who do you think is up there?"

"I guess whoever it is will have a good view of the fireworks tonight."

"I prefer the view from the surface. Tall buildings kind of make me sick now."

"Me too."

They ate at an open-air rotunda restaurant and made their way through the tropical drink menu as the sun went down, and when the hour grew late they went out to the plaza and looked up at the sky. The beautiful and endless array of stars that they had grown so accustomed to viewing from the deck of the *Mistical Reflection* was obscured by the light pollution from Atlantis. The crowd counted down to midnight and a grand display of fireworks erupted over the Royal Towers. Grey pulled Misty to him and kissed her.

"Happy New Year," he said.

"Happy New Year," she smiled back at him.

He held her hand and watched the beauty of her face light up in every explosive color, and he wondered if he could possibly love her more. They walked the beach again and swam back out to the yacht, still alone and dark, rocking in the waves as the fireworks and celebration faded away. Grey uncorked a bottle of champagne on the deck and they toasted the year ahead, both silently fearing what it would bring.

# 16

## Agents Descend

"Ladies and gentlemen, the captain has turned on the *Fasten Seatbelts* sign. We're beginning our descent into Nassau."

Agent Richter crunched on his last pretzel and poured the remaining salt from the bag into his mouth. "Wake up," he said, elbowing McGuinness in the window seat next to him. "We're almost there."

McGuinness sat up and looked out the window at the passing clouds. He took a sip from the plastic cup of water in front of him and handed it to the stewardess when she came by. Richter downed the rest of his Jack and Coke and crumpled his empty pretzel bag noisily and stuffed it into the empty cup and dropped it carelessly onto her cart. He leaned over the armrest into the aisle to watch her walk away.

"You check out that ass?" he said.

McGuinness shook his head and looked back out the window.

"Don't be such a stiff," said Richter. "You should drink sometimes. Loosen up. You might get laid once in a while."

"I've done enough of both. It's why I've been divorced twice."

"It's why I'm glad I'm a bachelor."

The plane flew into a cloud and the blue outside went white. Richter clutched his jacket as they jostled in their seats with the turbulence. After a moment the smooth clear sky returned.

"That gun won't do you any good up here," said McGuinness.

Richter took his hand out of his jacket and put it on his knee, bouncing nervously. He leaned forward and looked past McGuinness out the window. The waves below rolled together so close he wondered if the pilot planned a water landing.

"You know anything about this chick we're meeting?" he asked.

"A little."

"I don't know why they think we need an escort. Like we can't handle things on our own."

"It's their country. We don't have jurisdiction."

"We're the United Stated Federal Bureau of Investigation, and they're sending some island tour guide."

"She's an accomplished inspector of the Royal Bahamas Police force. Don't be so quick to discount people who may be able to help you. Have some professional courtesy and don't embarrass me."

The plane touched down and taxied off the runway to the jet bridge. The agents took their luggage from the compartment above their seats and waited as the rest of the passengers disembarked ahead of them. McGuinness watched them pass slowly in their shorts and sandals and smiles, blissfully unaware of the dangers that it seemed only he knew dwelt in the place they called paradise. A woman in plain clothes awaited them at the gate. Her youth and beauty surprised even McGuinness, the way the sun lit one side of her face white and left the other in shadow nearly the color of her long black braids. She greeted them with a bright smile.

"Welcome to the Bahamas," she said. "I'm Inspector Tatjana Thorne. I'll be keeping you company during your stay, so you'll have a local pair of eyes at your disposal."

"Pleasure to meet you, Inspector Thorne," said the older agent.

"And you," she replied. "Where to first, gentlemen?"

"Let's not waste any time," said Richter. "The call pinged from a tower on Paradise Island. Let's start there."

"You got it."

They followed Inspector Thorne to her waiting car and they drove through the city and across the bridge over Nassau Harbour. In the interest of the investigation, the FBI had incurred the expense of rooms at Atlantis where the agents changed into less conspicuous attire and left their bags. Richter took only a moment to glance out his window at the extravagant resort grounds below and the endless blue Caribbean water beyond, but McGuinness studied them closely from his room next door, memorizing the layout—the pathways—the buildings—the beaches. They met Inspector Thorne in the lobby and McGuinness pulled out his phone with the *WANTED* bulletin showing Grey and Misty's photos.

"I've sent a copy of this to your phone too," he said. "We'll start with resort security. Then reception personnel. Concierges. Restaurant staff. It's been over a week since the call, so I'm hoping we didn't lose them in the time it took to cut through the red tape. This is the first break we've had since they disappeared, so keep an eye out and a low profile. If they're still here we don't want to scare them off."

He eyed Richter.

"I'll be honest," said Inspector Thorne, "when I was told about your investigation, I was a little surprised. Is the Italian mafia still a relevant force in the US?"

"They don't have the political influence that they once did, and generally they make it a point to stay out of the limelight, so most people don't even know they're there. But yes, they're still around."

"And these two—they work for a mob boss who turns up dead, and they just vanish?"

"Not before we had a chance to talk to them," replied Richter.

"No phone records? Credit card transactions? Bank withdrawals? Hotel reservations?"

"No. Their phones haven't been used, bank accounts haven't been touched, no credit transactions in their names. Even their cars are still at their house. We were stalled until this slip."

"So they have help?"

"Maybe," said Richter.

"Someone inside the mob?" asked Thorne.

McGuinness remained silent.

"Or they aren't who we think they are," said the young agent. "Why don't you two stick together? Give me a call from the security office and let me know if you get anything new. I'd like to look around a little bit."

"I know it's tempting," said Inspector Thorne, "but don't spend too much time on the beach. Wouldn't want you to burn while you're in my care."

McGuinness smiled.

"I think I can handle myself," said Richter.

As McGuinness and Thorne departed for the security office to brief their personnel, Richter followed the same paths of the Lost City that Grey and Misty had walked and stood in the same sand on the same beach watching the same blue tide crash with its relentless rhythm and sweep back within itself. He squinted to focus on the sails offshore, watching them move slowly across the horizon just beyond his reach. He examined every one of the dozens of faces he passed recognizing none. He stopped to observe a group of college-aged girls on winter break as they pranced dripping from the surf to lie out on lounge chairs, the oil on their tanned skin shining in the sun. Then he left the beach and crossed the bridge over the lagoon and passed the pool and the shadow of the Royal Towers, discovering the dark and subtle entrance to The Dig aquarium. The same catacombs that Grey and Misty had wandered just days before led Richter into that terrifying blue world of predators and prey beneath the surface. Bottom-dwelling crustaceans crept under purple neon lights and green eels peered from holes in stone walls with mouths wide open screaming silently. Sharks swam just inches from the faces of tourists in the glass tunnel beneath Predator Lagoon. Richter shivered in the damp chill and followed the path to a stairway that led to the rotunda pavilion at the surface where he took a seat at the bar.

"Welcome to the Lagoon Bar and Grill," said the bartender. "What can I get for you?"

"Jack and Coke."

The bartender returned with his drink, and Richter took out his phone. "Have you ever seen either of these people?" he asked, showing him side-by-side photos of Grey and Misty.

"Sure. They were here a few nights ago."

Richter set his phone on the bar and leaned closer. "You're sure?"

"Definitely. You don't forget a face like hers."

"Right. Do you remember which night?"

"New Years Eve. They were here for the fireworks. I don't think they were staying here though."

"Why's that?"

The bartender pointed to the Atlantis guest wristband on Richter's arm.

"They weren't wearing those."

Richter picked up his phone and called McGuinness who answered immediately.

"You two still with security?"

"Just left."

"Anything good? Surveillance footage?"

"Tons of it; that's the problem. There are hundreds of cameras all over this place running twenty-four hours a day. We need a time and place to start."

"I've got one," said Richter.

"You're kidding."

"Just good instincts. First guy I talked to was this bartender at the—" he looked down at the menu in front of him, "the Lagoon Bar and Grill. They were here on New Years Eve watching the fireworks."

"Stay there," said McGuinness. "We're coming to you."

Richter sat back and sipped on his Jack and Coke, watching the tourists drifting past. Less than five minutes later McGuinness and Thorne swiftly but discreetly slipped into the shadow of the dome roof and sat down next to Richter at the bar. Thorne spun on the stool and faced the lagoon.

"What else did he say?" she asked.

"I was waiting for you," replied Richter.

The bartender appeared again.

"Drinks for you two?"

"No," said McGuinness, showing him the photos of Grey and Misty again. "You saw this couple the other night?"

"Yes."

"Did they look any different than they do in these pictures? Different hairstyles? Anything?"

"Yeah, her hair was a little darker, and his was shorter. And he had a bit of a beard. They were a little more tan," he laughed. "It's the Caribbean, you know."

"How did they pay? Cash? Credit card?"

"I don't remember. Why are you asking all these questions?"

Richter took his wallet from his pocket and dropped his credit card on the counter along with his FBI credentials.

"I see," said the bartender. "They must have done something pretty bad for the American FBI to come all this way."

"Maybe," replied McGuinness. "So, cash or credit?"

"Let me check."

He took Richter's credit card from the bar and went to the register. The two agents watched the computer screen as the bartender scanned through records and Inspector Thorne kept watch. The bartender returned with Richter's card and bill and the transaction report for New Years Eve.

"You'll have to run through them on your own," said the bartender. "I don't remember their names or what they drank, but I'm sure you can figure it out."

The bartender stepped away as Richter ran his finger down the list.

"Well they weren't stupid enough to use cards in their own names."

"We knew that," said McGuinness.

"There are a few cash transactions here."

"It's fine. We have a place to start. There's a camera pointed right at us, and it looks like it covers most of the restaurant. We'll pull the surveillance footage for that night and compare it against these transactions. If they used a card we're golden."

Thorne turned back to the agents.

"Let's hit the security office again, then we can head back to the station."

"Could be a late one, Tatjana," said Richter. "You up for it?"

Inspector Thorne smiled.

"Always, Robert."

Richter's head slipped from its resting place in the palm of his hand propped on the desk and then jolted back into a state of alertness. He rubbed his eyes and looked out the window of the empty police station at the night sky. The towers of Atlantis glowed orange in the distance. Red and green boat lights crossed paths on the horizon. He turned back toward the computer screen upon which both Conrad McGuinness and Tatjana Thorne had fixed their gazes, the room silent save for the hum of fluorescent lighting.

"How far in are we?" he asked.

"About three hours," replied McGuinness.

"Still no sign of them?"

"You bored or something?"

"Just tired. It's been a long day."

Inspector Thorne smiled at the image on the monitor.

"Get used to it," said McGuinness. "Get yourself some coffee."

Richter stood up and took a lap around the office. He went to the window and opened it and breathed a breath of the cool Bahamian night. His heavy eyelids fell, and he leaned his head against the glass.

"There!" said Inspector Thorne, startling Richer awake again.

"Yes," whispered Agent McGuinness. "Welcome, Mr. Cavanaugh."

Richter came back around behind them to watch.

"OK, they're just sitting down at the bar. Mark the time on the video. Now we watch what they order and when they pay the bill and compare it with the transaction report. Let's fast forward a bit."

"Got it," said Richter. "You think they have any idea what they've gotten into?"

"Put it this way," replied McGuinness, "if they had known what they were getting into they never would have taken the job in the first place. Based on my experience with the Mancini family, they're screwed whether they were involved in the boss's death or not."

"How long were you in with the mob?" asked Thorne.

"Six years with the Zanetti family. Never with Mancini, but the—" he paused, "another agency asked us to take credit for taking him down because they didn't want their involvement made public. I got to know Salvatore Mancini during the investigation though, as well as anyone would ever want to know that man." He shuddered. "He was the coldest person I've ever met. The world is better off without him. Anyway, while Sal was locked up his family joined forces with Gianni Zanetti, but that all fell apart when he was released in two thousand eleven. Sal and Gianni didn't get along so well, and the empire was split. It's been a point of contention for both of them, to put it lightly."

"Alright," said Richter, calling their attention back to the computer screen. "They're paying the bill."

"Eleven forty-seven," said Thorne.

Richter looked at the transaction list. "Here it is," he said, dropping his finger onto the page. "We've got you now, Grey Cavanaugh. Or should I say *Stephen Johnson?*"

"Let's watch it again."

# 17

## Loose Lips Sink Ships

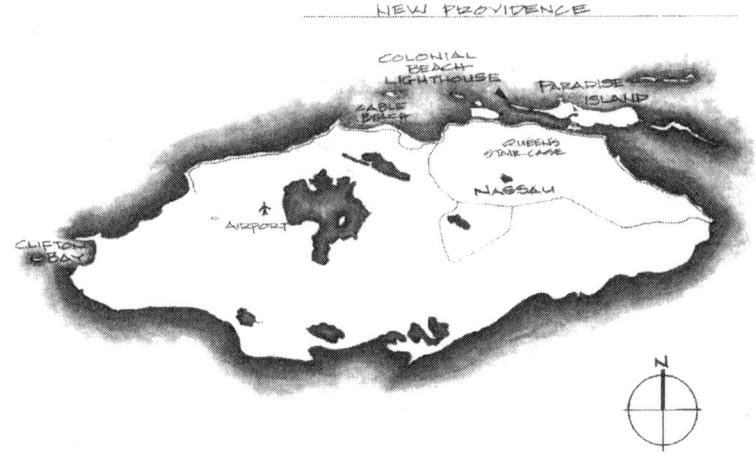

"**A**uthorities say the fugitives disappeared over two months ago and are now believed to be somewhere on New Providence or Paradise Island. They are going by the names of Stephen Johnson and Melissa Cruise. If you encounter them, notify the police immediately and do not approach them. They are considered dangerous."

A trail of sand lined the sidewalk behind four bare feet as Grey and Misty ran from the beachside market with its televisions and witnesses. They ran with their sandals swinging from their hands. The weight of each swift step crashed on the pavement with the shattering significance of the damning words spoken by the news reporter behind mirror images of the two staring back at them. They shielded their faces from passersby, their eyes scanning the concrete patterns sweeping beneath them. The colorful buildings and traffic of Nassau blurred in their periphery.

"How did they find us?" Grey muttered.

Misty was silent, her eyes fixed on the rhythm of her feet falling between the cracks of the pavement.

"We have to get out of here," said Grey. "We have to get back to the boat."

"What if they've found it already?"

"We'll cross that bridge when we get to it. Right now it's our best option. It's not safe here anymore."

The teal sea sparkled in glimpses between the buildings. Palm shadows swayed across their path, fronds hissing in the wind. Misty felt the spray of Grey's sweat from his arm beside her and she took his hand to slow him down.

"We shouldn't run," she said. "It'll call attention."

They slowed to a brisk walk. The cruise ships of Nassau Harbour came into view on the left as they turned onto Bay Street and the towers of Atlantis beckoned just beyond.

Grey looked directly north across the blue harbor to the lighthouse on the western leg of Paradise Island where the *Mistical Reflection* awaited just on the other side.

"We could swim," he said. "It has to be faster than going all the way to the bridge."

"But all the boats. It's dangerous."

"More dangerous than getting caught?"

An engine roared and they looked to the right as an old Jeep tore out of a side street and screeched to a stop beside them.

"Get in," came an unexpectedly welcome voice from a familiar face. "Now."

"Tobias."

Misty put a foot on the tire and leapt over the rear fender into the back seat and Grey jumped into the front. They held fast to the roll bars as Tobias hit the gas and turned onto the next street, back into the grid of downtown Nassau.

"Where are you going?" Grey demanded. "Our boat's anchored off Paradise Island."

"You don't want to go that way," said Tobias. "Everyone knows your faces now. You'll never get across the bridge."

"What happened? How did they find us?"

"You were supposed to get rid of the cell phone."

"We haven't used it," Grey insisted.

Tobias looked into the rear view mirror at Misty.

"I did," she said reluctantly. "I called my parents on Christmas."

"Damn it," said Grey, shaking his head. "Why did we have a traceable phone?"

"It's just a burner phone. Your names aren't on it, but it's not untraceable, which is why you were only supposed to be talking to Declan, and only on the satphone. The FBI had Misty's family bugged, waiting for an opportunity like this. Once the call came through they traced it back here. Give it to me."

Tobias reached his open palm around to the back seat. Misty took the phone from her pocket and handed it to him. Grey watched his eyes alternate between the road and the screen as he drove quickly but discreetly through the streets, both passengers holding tight to stay in their seats.

"No photos or texts," said Tobias. "That's good. This will be clean."

He slowed down as he turned into a neighborhood of shanty homes and vacant buildings with boarded windows. A group of young men stood on a street corner. Their conversation ceased and their faces turned suspicious, eyeing the approaching Jeep. Tobias took out a handkerchief and wiped his fingerprints off the phone, then held it out toward them as he pulled up to the curb.

"Free cell phone," he said.

The young men looked at each other, then down both cross streets and back at Tobias.

"You want it or not?"

One of the men hesitantly stepped forward and snatched the phone from Tobias's outstretched hand.

He dropped the clutch and hit the gas, and they sped off again.

"That will throw the FBI off for a bit. Now we get you two out of here."

They drove west until the buildings of Nassau spread out and shrank behind them. The shadow of a Cessna passed across the Jeep as it flew low overhead. Misty watched as it touched down on the runway just south of the road and she wondered if the plan was to escape by airplane, but Tobias drove on past the airport. Minutes later he turned off the paved road and onto a rough dirt path, barreling into the tropical Bahamian woods and kicking up a cloud of dust like an impervious wall behind them. The blue sky nearly vanished behind the tropical green ceiling.

In a clearing up ahead the deep blue ocean emerged beyond a vacant beach that spanned the horizon. A three-seated jetboat rested at the edge of the surf. The Jeep stopped in the sand at the bow of the boat and Tobias stepped out, pulling a black bag from under his seat. "Let's go," he said. Grey and Misty followed. Tobias tossed the bag into the boat and they pushed it out into the waves and jumped in. The motor rumbled beneath them as the hull spun sharply and headed north, passing Clifton Bay and cutting northeast around Nygard Cay to follow the coastline. They glided across the waves with such speed that the boat seemed never to touch the water beneath.

"Empty your pockets," Tobias yelled over the sound of the engine. "The identification, credit cards—it's all trash now. Replacements are in this bag. Money has been moved. Account numbers have been changed. Cash only from now on. The cards and cell phone are only for emergency. The FBI is dangerously close, and if they know where you are, so does the mob. No more slips. This can't happen again."

The boat swept past Discovery Island off Cable Beach and the lighthouse of Paradise Island came into view. Beside it was the *Mistical Reflection*, untouched.

"So what do we do now?" asked Grey.

"Get the hell out of here as fast as you can. Then call Declan."

He sped a short distance past the *Mistical Reflection*, scanning the beach for watchful eyes, then came about and slowly approached. They tied the jetboat up to the yacht and all three climbed aboard.

"Either of you ever shot a gun before?" asked Tobias, dropping the black bag on a seat and unzipping it.

"Yes," said Grey.

"Once," said Misty.

"Good," replied Tobias as he pulled a pistol from the bag. "This is a nineteen eleven. It's a forty-five caliber, classic design and still the best on the market. Guaranteed to stop anyone in their tracks. And listen," he said, handing the gun to Grey, "don't shoot the FBI. That would be very bad for you. This is for the mob's henchmen."

"You think we'll need it?"

Tobias sighed. "These people are very persistent. They won't stop until they get what they want, and right now they want you. Just keep it handy, and quit acting like you're on vacation. Your lives are in danger. You need to pay more attention."

He hopped back over the side into the jetboat and untied it from the *Mistical Reflection*. "Good luck," he said. The engine started and he sped off leaving the yacht rocking in his wake.

Grey and Misty weighed anchor and raised the sails as the sun began to set. They set off toward the darkening eastern sky, its stars beginning to shine through the passing clouds, hoping to find refuge in the coming night. A cool wind whipped across the deck drawing them deeper into the lonely abyss of unanswered questions. Grey dialed Declan on the satellite phone as he and Misty watched the Lost City pass for the last time.

"Grey."

"Dad."

"Are you OK?"

"Yes. We're both OK."

"Looks like you've worn out your welcome in the Bahamas."

"Seems so," Grey replied.

"We need to put some distance between you and the FBI. Are you up for a sail?"

"Yes."

"Good. Head down to Tortola."

"It will be days before we're out of Bahamian waters, and now they're looking for us. What if we're stopped by the Defense Force?"

"The RBDF has been redirected," said Declan. "They'll be patrolling elsewhere for the next few days. Just move quickly. Tobias gave you new identification. Check in with BVI Customs when you get to Tortola."

"Dad."

"Yes."

"I need to know what you know."

Declan paused a moment before he spoke, sounds of distant traffic behind his silence. "You're going to find out eventually," he said, "so you might as well hear it from me. By now you know a little bit about your former employer, Salvatore Mancini. As far as the public was concerned, it was the FBI that arrested him in nineteen ninety-one. What you don't know is that, in reality, it was the Agency that took him down. He was laundering money for an international terrorist enterprise based out of Libya. I worked with your new friend, Special Agent McGuinness, to make it happen. It was my last official assignment with the Agency."

"You know McGuinness?" asked Grey, the phone in his hand beginning to shake. "The agent who's trying to arrest me for murder?"

"I do."

"Murder of a mafia boss that you two took down together."

"Yes."

"And I just happened to be chosen by that same mafia boss to design a building for him. That's a lot of coincidences."

"There are no coincidences," said Declan. "Mancini knew exactly who you were."

"Does McGuinness know what's going on? Is he in on all of this?"

"I don't think so. Not yet."

"We should have just stayed," Grey insisted. "We should have just talked to him to begin with. Now I look guilty, and I dragged Misty into this mess."

She moved closer to him and took his hand. Grey breathed in the perfume of her hair blowing in the cool wind, tickling his cheek.

"Grey, listen," said Declan. "We're not worried about the feds. It doesn't matter if you're guilty or not. You're the fall guy. The people who set you up can't have you talking about what you know."

"I don't know anything!" Grey yelled, slamming his fist into the gunwale and startling Misty.

"You may know more than you think you do, but it doesn't matter. They won't risk it."

"Who are they?"

"Grey—" a gust of wind on the other end muffled Declan's voice. "I have to go. Remember, no more cell phones, no calls to anyone but me. Loose lips sink ships."

Grey sat at the helm holding the wheel steady with one hand and Misty's with the other. She sat beside him, quietly gazing at the lights of Atlantis shrinking where their wake disappeared into a glistening pink and orange sunset sea. A bead of sweat dripped down her forehead as her eyes followed the horizon, its bright warm line turning cold and dark, yet strangely inviting beneath the starry sky. Soon morning would come and all of those lights on the horizon would be gone, and a new world would emerge from the blue.

# 18

## An Ice Cold Man, a Frozen White Night

Declan set the phone down beside him as the frozen winter wind whistled across the rooftop of The Drake Hotel, wiping away his footprints in the snow. He looked west toward the orange sun, soon to fall behind the Chicago skyline as he admired its beauty, all of those structures representing decades—generations of architectural design from wood and stone to steel and glass. Then he peered down the scope of his Kivaari .338 Lapua Magnum across Lake Shore Drive, beyond the white-cloaked Oak Street Beach, and into the cabin of a luxury yacht floating all alone on the lake where his crosshairs intersected on Gianni Zanetti's chest. He switched the safety off and slowly moved his finger to the trigger and took a calm, deep breath.

"I could take you right now, you son of a bitch," he muttered. "Lucky for you I still need you alive."

He breathed again and switched the safety on and set the rifle aside. Beneath the white hood camouflaged with the snow he turned on the receiver to his earpiece and listened. The radio signal transmitted from the bug on Zanetti's yacht was as clear as if he were there inside, face to face with the man himself. There were nine of those bugs throughout the vessel, placement of which had made the previous night long and cold and wet, an almost comfortably nostalgic territory for an operative of Declan's experience. His warm breath dissipated into the frozen air, disguised by the steam of the hotel's HVAC exhaust vent beside him.

He steadied his binoculars and watched through the yacht's windows and listened as Zanetti puffed on his cigar, the hiss barely audible as it burned down. The windows glowed a dim orange from inside the cabin, highlighted against the deep purple hull melting into the lake as the sun vanished behind the city. Shadows of henchmen in overcoats paced the deck. There were at least six that Declan counted.

Inside the phone rang. He watched Zanetti rise and walk across the cabin to answer at the bar.

"Yes?" he said, setting his cigar in a crystal ashtray and pouring a glass of wine. He stroked his shining bald head.

"Sir," said the hesitant voice on the other end. "They're gone."

"What?" Zanetti yelled. "How is that possible? The FBI led you right to them!"

"They figured it out. And they have help."

"I don't want to hear your excuses. If you don't find them, and soon, you'll have to answer for it."

"Yes, sir."

"And remember, it has to look like an accident. If the feds find them with bullet holes in them it doesn't do me any good."

Zanetti slammed the phone back into its cradle and downed the glass of wine. He put the cigar back in his mouth and began to pace within the cabin. He went to the window and cupped his hands over his brow to peer out, searching the skyline, pausing as his gaze fell upon The Drake. His eyes looked straight into Declan's on the rooftop as if he knew from where the shot would come, but he could see nothing. Declan looked straight back through his binoculars, concealed by the steam and the frost and the night.

Zanetti stepped back from the window and went to the bar and poured another glass of wine, and then he sat in his armchair and gazed out at the frozen night. Declan listened to the silence from within the vessel, watching the man adjust his position in the armchair, watching the subtle red ripples in his glass when he trembled as if contemplating his fate. Zanetti picked up a remote control and pressed a button, and through his earpiece Declan heard *Moonlight Sonata* playing softly in the cabin, each beautifully mysterious note drawing him deeper into his haunting past where it all began. A light snow began to fall upon the city and the cold, dark lake.

The silhouette of a henchman crossed the rear deck of the yacht and entered the cabin. He shook the snow off of his overcoat and blew into the palms of his hands and rubbed them together. Zanetti puffed on his cigar and looked to the man in the doorway.

"Anything?"

"No, Mr. Zanetti. There's nobody else on the water in this weather."

"Keep looking. I don't like surprises."

"That's why you're staying on the yacht. If anyone comes out here we'll know it."

"Don't be so sure," said Zanetti. "The Mancini family is ruthless."

"We could hit them first."

"No. Going on the offensive will make it look like I'm behind it. Sal did this to himself when he gave Grey Cavanaugh reason to kill him. The longer this goes on, though, the more I think Cavanaugh was in on Sal's plan all along, and maybe that Misty girl too."

"Then why would Sal fire them and risk a leak?"

"I don't know, none of it makes sense, but I'll feel better when they're at the bottom of the ocean. Normal people don't know how to disappear the way they did, and the timing of it all just as I'm getting into this new venture—if they know about our Mexican partners they could ruin the whole deal. I can't have that. There's too much money on the table, not to mention my life. If this deal goes sour, well, that's one group whose bad side I never want to be on. It's a delicate situation we're in. Once this blows over and the Mancini family is convinced I had nothing to do with Sal's murder and our business partners are none the wiser to this whole mess, then I can move back in, but for now we need to keep our distance."

The henchman nodded and turned to make his way back out onto the deck. From the rooftop Declan watched Zanetti burn down his cigar and finish his glass of wine, then fall asleep in his armchair under the still burning lights to the sound of Vivaldi's "Winter."

# 19

## Pirates of the Caribbean

The wind was warm as it cut between the sails of the *Mistical Reflection* cruising along the sparkling surface of the deep blue Caribbean Sea. Grey sat at the helm watching Misty's cheeks glowing in the rising sun. He pulled a tricorne hat from below the seat and placed it snugly on his head shading his eyes. His shirt blew like a cape in the wind. Misty looked at him and laughed.

"Where did you get that hat, Grey?"

"Picked it up at the gift shop at Atlantis."

"You look ridiculous. And sexy. You and your pirate ship, Captain Cavanaugh."

"Arg," he said, taking a cigar from the box beside him. He flipped his Zippo open and cupped his hand to shield the flame from the wind and his palm lit up orange with each burning drag. He snapped the lighter shut and took the cigar from his mouth and looked at her.

"We're the real pirates of the Caribbean," he said.

She laughed again and rolled her eyes at him, and suddenly an expression of disbelief washed across her face.

"Look!" she said, pointing behind him. Grey turned and looked from the helm and beheld a sight to the northwest that left him speechless. In their wake a pod of bottlenose dolphins drew upon the yacht, leaping from the water, arching through the air, and diving back beneath the surface. White water trailed behind dorsal fins and flukes painting patterns across the horizon.

"How many do you think there are?" she asked.

"Must be dozens," Grey replied. He eased the mainsheet slightly to let the pod gain. They came alongside the gunwales, leaping and diving so close that the streams from their glistening gray skin showered the teak deck turning it dark. Misty reached her hand over the side where a beak broke through the spray and affectionately tapped her fingertips before falling into the blue again. Then another did the same.

"They're beautiful," she yelled over the ubiquitous splashing on all sides of the hull cutting through the waves. A white mist surrounded them with the rich smell of the morning sea. As Grey slowed the yacht and the sails luffed the pod of dolphins slowed with them, circling and playing and passing beneath the hull to emerge again on the other side. Misty flipped the lid of her seat open and sifted through the life preservers and snorkeling equipment stored in its compartment, and she donned her fins and goggles and dove into the crystal clear water. Grey lowered the sails and snuffed his cigar and followed her.

Beneath the surface the whole world changed. The colors of the reef shone vivid and bright in purples and reds and yellows lit by the curtains of sunbeams dancing against a blue eternity. A school of angelfish decorated in gold and indigo coral camouflage approached curiously and then darted away in instant synchronicity as Misty reached to touch them. She and Grey drifted with fluid ease among the myriad of life obscured by the waves and hidden from the world above. The dolphins played, whistling and clicking and whirling in a jubilant performance for their visitors who swam alongside them, mimicking their graceful flow. Grey watched Misty, and he thought that perhaps the only thing happier than a dolphin in the wild was a person swimming among them, separated from all of the world's troubles, if only for a few moments. Even his own qualms with the events that had led them to this place suddenly seemed trivial, and all he felt was love— love for the sea, love for the earth and every natural element within and upon it, and most of all love for Misty. He swam beside her and took her hand and pressed his mask against hers to gaze into her eyes. They surfaced for a breath, and when they submerged again the dolphins were gone.

Shadows of clouds passed over the deck and the azure waves as the *Mistical Reflection* continued to sail southeast. Six days had passed since they had left Nassau, and they had seen no sign of the RBDF or anyone else on their tail. Grey examined the GPS at the helm.

"We're almost out of Bahamian waters," he called to Misty at the bow, too focused on her yoga meditation to respond. He watched her as she slid from lotus into hare and then downward dog and he admired the view. "Ready about!" he said, and she fell through her vinyasa flow to chaturanga as they tacked and the jib swept across her back. She raised her head and looked forward across the bow.

"What are those islands?" she asked, gliding into a warrior pose and fighting for balance as the yacht rode crests and troughs.

"Turks and Caicos," he replied.

She came down to the deck again and flowed into upward bow. Her hair fell between her toned arms and she looked back toward him at the helm.

"You're just as pretty upside down," he said.

"Thank you," she smiled. "So are you."

Grey cocked his head to the side. "I'm not upside down."

She lay flat on her back and rolled over into cobra. "Not anymore," she laughed.

He watched her eyes fall to her hands and pause for a moment before rising again to meet his, and he felt at the same time both joy that she could still love him after everything that she had given up for him and sadness that it seemed the life they had dreamt up together would never be. She stood and walked along the gunwale from the bow back toward the helm where he stood at the wheel, and she kissed his cheek before picking up a book and sitting beside him. She stretched out on the seat, adjusting for maximum exposure to the sun.

"Do you still want to marry me?" she asked.
"You know I do."
"Promise?"
"Of course."

She watched him quietly for a while, and then she rolled over and opened her book. Grey wondered what it was she was reading, but he did not want to disturb her. She looked so peaceful. She deserved some peace, he thought.

He took a southern heading, bearing toward Hispaniola, the shoreline of which he hoped to see by dawn the next day. A chain of white clouds lay on the horizon where the island would emerge. The vastness of the sea was breathtaking. There was no end to it—only the occasional interruption of earth that protruded in colors other than blue and shapes other than horizontal lines.

He sat beside Misty and reached over the side and let his fingertips graze the water passing by. He cupped his hand beneath the surface, and then he ran it through his hair, letting the saltwater drip down his forehead, and the breeze turned cold. He stood again and wrapped his hands around the smooth wood of the ship's wheel. Misty lay on the seat beside him looking down at her book with her back to the sun, and he saw a tear fall onto the page.

"Misty," he said, sitting beside her again, "what's wrong?"

"Nothing," she sobbed.

"Why are you crying?"

"The book."

"The book?"

"It's so sad."

He sighed. "Why do you read that crap?"

"It makes me feel human."

"Don't you want to read stories that take you on adventures to exciting foreign lands and leave the real world behind?"

"I have you for that," she said. "Sometimes truth is stranger than fiction."

"Who said that?"

"Mark Twain."

"That's my kind of author," said Grey as he looked up at the horizon. "Him and Jules Verne. There's still nothing like *Twenty Thousand Leagues Under the Sea*. Or, how about Herman Melville's *Moby Dick?* Daniel Defoe's *Robinson Crusoe.* Yann Martel's *Life of Pi*. Those are great stories."

"You're in love," she said, wiping her eyes.

"With you? Yes."

"With the ocean."

"Well, that too."

"There's something you're missing about all of those stories."

"What's that?" he asked.

"They all have some pretty rough spots."

"So does ours."

"And they're all about shipwrecks."

Well into the night a subtle artificial glow grew on the horizon ahead. Grey looked past the wheel and admired the large compass inlay sprawled across the decking. His gaze followed the plank lines to the mast and up the white sail to where it ended at the edge of the black sky. Then it fell to Misty, sleeping quietly beside him. The hull struck a large wave and she stirred, but she did not wake. She was just as beautiful in the moonlight, and he wondered how she could sleep so easily and so deeply. She slept the way she loved.

The black bag of lies lay on the seat beneath her feet. Carefully, so as not to wake her, Grey lifted her legs and pulled the bag out from under them and laid them to rest again gently. He set the bag down on the seat beside him and quietly unzipped it. He pulled out the pistol and examined it in his hand. The moonlight streaked along its blued lines in such a delicate way that it was almost beautiful, and he thought back to his training as a child that had seemed so purposeless then. He pulled the slide back halfway and peered through the ejection port into the empty chamber and pulled further until it clicked. Then he eased his tension and watched a round glide from the magazine into the chamber, and the slide snapped into place leaving the hammer cocked.

Waves struck the hull with predictable rhythm in the steady night wind, and Grey looked at Misty lying innocently at his side. He watched her sleep with the gun in his hand. He was dangerous—as dangerous as the FBI thought him to be—as dangerous as those who hunted him. He looked up at the full moon. "How little you know," he muttered, and he pointed the gun to the sky, aligning the glowing target with his sights. "Come and get me," he grinned. Slowly he set the hammer back in place and stored the pistol back in the bag.

When Grey slept, Misty took the helm and kept their course steady into the easterly wind, but he slept little. Rarely did his hands leave the wooden wheel and the nylon lines that maintained control of perhaps the one thing he still could. Rarely did his feet leave the stage belonging to the captain of the elegant vessel born of his own imagination. The *Mistical Reflection* sailed past San Juan three days later. Misty sat on the deck with her back against the butterfly hatches and her feet dangling loosely over the side. Her toes grazed the surface of the blue, dipping beneath the crest of each cold wave washing past. She watched the coastline, the skyscrapers, remembering their life in the city that seemed so much longer than three months gone.

"Grey," she said.

"Yes."

"Have you remembered anything else about that night in Chicago?"

"Nothing I haven't already told you."

"Don't you think that's strange?"

"I drank a lot," he said. "Maybe it was the absinthe. Maybe someone put something in it. I don't know."

"It just seems—I don't know—convenient. To an outsider I mean."

"An alibi would be convenient."

"I guess."
"Are you asking me if I did it?"
"I wouldn't ask you that."
"Doesn't mean you don't want to."

# 20

## Deals With God

A bell clanged with hollow dullness, the vaguely familiar sound echoing bizarrely from the edge of the jungle. In the shade of the thick green ceiling, its patterns constantly transforming in the breeze, the floor was nearly black allowing no sight of what lurked within to anyone on the outside. Where the jungle ended the beach began, its fine off-white softness sparkling in the sun. There Grey and Misty sat peering into the tropical woodland, curiously seeking the source of the strange noise in an otherwise deserted scene. Then came the sound of footsteps crunching sluggishly across fallen fronds and sticks, drawing nearer to the beach.

A lone cow emerged from the palm trees and into the sun, the bell hanging from a rope around its neck clanging with each step as it casually walked through the sand in front of Grey and Misty. For a few moments they watched, bemused. The cow paid them no mind. It crossed in front of the bright blue horizon and disappeared again into the jungle on the opposite side of the beach.

"Huh," said Grey.

"That's strange. I wonder where she came from."

"And where she's going."

The beach was secluded—a small crescent bay bordered on one side by a colossal cliff peninsula, the other by a headland of boulders that rolled into the sea, heavily wooded volcanic hills behind, and the endless blue beyond the sand. Nestled between the beach and the jungle was a small house where Declan had arranged for them to stay for the foreseeable future. Tall palm trees arched over its roof concealing it almost entirely from every angle. There were no locks on its doors, there was no air conditioning, but it was designed with the expectation that its doors and windows would be left open to draw a draft through the rooms and keep them cool. There was little of value inside to protect. Besides, no lock would deter those who sought them. The shower was an outdoor space with a trellis overhead bound by stone retaining walls at the edge of the jungle, and a worn wooden deck wrapped around the two sides of the house that faced the beach. The *Mistical Reflection* remained anchored in the bay.

The water was shallow a long way out and bright turquoise and clear as the air. The beach was so secret that even the birds rarely visited, but the fish were plenty and colorful. Schools of them driven in by the tide remained within their newfound safe haven, hidden away from the dangerous world outside. Sailboats and ships crossed the horizon between the cliff and the boulders, but none ever made their way in, nor did any car ever venture down the dirt road from the hills, nor did any person ever come out of the jungle. It seemed as though Grey and Misty would never be found.

In a shed behind the house a Jeep had been left for their use. It was covered in a sheet and had not been driven in such a long time that the tires had to be filled with air and the engine with fresh oil and the tank with fuel, but it started up without trouble. They left the safety of the beach only every week or two to replenish their stock of food and drinking water. The drive to the Road Town market was beautiful but treacherous—a steep unpaved path barely wide enough for one vehicle that wound through the jungle and along the edge of a cliff and offered spectacular views of the surrounding isles. Wildlife and farm animals wandered freely throughout the island of Tortola, an occasional herd of goats or wild boar in the roadway requiring that Grey and Misty wait their turn. They were not hurried.

Weeks turned to months. Grey began fishing to pass the time, pulling bizarre and colorful tropical fish out of the ocean and watching them flop around on the yacht's deck, their gills opening and closing, gasping for breath until they finally ceased to move. "It's strange," he said. "Fishing is the only sport I know of that shares its name with the creatures being slain. We're being humanned." They would bring his catch in and grill it whole over a fire on the beach and pick it apart like savages in the Caribbean sun.

"I never knew you to fish before," said Misty. "Why now?"

"Why not?" he said. "I have the time. And I don't like driving to town for food we can get right here. Besides, I can't get used to driving on the left side of the road. It would make more sense if the wheel was on the right."

As much as they loved the island, without the distraction of the chase both began to miss their work. They were itching to design, filling notebooks with fresh building layouts and perspective drawings. They sat quietly beside each other at the bar in the kitchen facing out across the beach, diligently drafting new concepts derived from the island's beautiful nature. Both thought often of the Star Silo project, the way it at once celebrated the urban history of its surroundings and paved the way to a bright future for the city of St. Louis, but the more Grey thought the more vexed he was by Misty's question about the building plans, specifically the top two floors. He had been too stubborn to listen before, to consider the possibility that those inconsistencies she had discovered could in fact hold the very secret that had put their lives in danger.

"Misty," he said at last.

"Yes."

"Tell me again what you saw in the plans. The Star Silo."

"The hidden rooms?"

"Yes."

She turned to a blank page in her notebook and began to draw. She sketched the layout of the penthouse offices from memory as Grey watched. The exterior walls matched, the windows matched, the doorways, the elevator shaft, the restrooms. Everything was exactly as he had designed it, and just before finishing the last few walls she stopped and looked at him.

"That's it," she said.

"What about here? Around the back of the elevator shaft."

"That's the hidden room. The plan is laid out in such a way that you would never notice the missing space unless you were looking for it. It's the same on both floors, with double-thick concrete and steel plate walls. The amount of power they have running to it is crazy. And here—" she pointed the pencil at an inconspicuous wall from the large room into a small adjacent office, "this is the secret passageway. The bookcases."

"What about the elevator shaft?"

"What about it?" she asked.

"The elevators have dual doors on opposite sides, but only the south door should open at these two floors."

"Oh," she said, looking down at the page. "Yes. On the plans I saw, the freight elevator opened to both the south lobby and the hidden room to the north."

"OK," he said, "So the question is why. What are they using hidden rooms for?"

"Well, it's the mob. Counterfeiting? Stockpiling cash? Smuggling drugs? Weapons?"

"Any of those things. The freight elevator goes to the roof, and there's a helicopter pad up there. They could easily bring in and send out shipments undetected, and this building would be the perfect front."

She shook her head. "And they couldn't do it without us," she said.

"Both of us. Misty, you were the only one who knew these secrets, and Mancini had a vendetta against my father. I don't think he was going to let either of us live. He didn't want us talking because he knew we'd catch on."

"But surely his own death wasn't part of his plan."

"No," he said. "It wasn't."

She looked at him.

"Grey—"

"There has to be someone else in on this. Someone Mancini didn't account for. Someone who's still pulling strings."

"Who?"

"I don't know."

They sailed to the baths at Virgin Gorda and slept on the *Mistical Reflection* for a week. They swam in the natural pools and explored the grottos beneath massive granite boulders where sunlight only just peered between the cracks and the air and the water were cool and still. They watched the hot red sunrise each morning and cool purple sunset each night, and every day was more or less the same. Then they sailed back to their secluded bay on Tortola that was just as they had left it.

Misty was glad to have dry land where she could run again—not away from anything or anyone, but for herself. In the jungle hills around the bay her bare feet left new tracks in the untouched ground, and her tracks became beaten paths the more she ran. Even during the day the thick green canopy kept the forest floor dark and cool. The palm trees and boulders and cliffs became as familiar as the street corners back home, and she fell in love with the wild landscape of the island. Miles upon miles she ran through the brush, her feet becoming calloused by the rough, but she did not mind. She did not mind the slopes or the rocks or the thorns or the rain. Every obstacle made her stronger—more capable and more determined—and when she broke out of the woods and into the light at the beach she would look each time to the horizon and catch her breath, watching the *Mistical Reflection* peacefully waiting at anchor.

Without his work, Grey grew bored and began running with Misty to relieve the tension and anxiety of complacency. On days that they did not run they climbed the boulders that bounded one side of the bay or swam from the beach out to the yacht where they sometimes slept nights on the deck just because they could. They watched the stars and the moon light up the sky so brightly that the horizon and the island were always visible in black silhouettes. The Milky Way looked like a crack in the night.

"What if we could peel it open and peek through to the other side?" said Misty. "What do you think we'd find?"

"More stars."

"But the view would be different. Like the ocean. You look east at any given time, then look west. It's always different."

"And it's always beautiful," said Grey.

"Yes. It's beautiful."

"And terrifyingly unfathomable. How small we are. How little control we have."

"Why didn't we sleep out like this at home?"

"The stars don't look like this at home."

"Do you ever wonder how we got here?" she asked.

"We sailed here."

"I mean this life. The families we're born into, the places we live, the people we meet. Successes and failures. Gains and losses. Friends and enemies. Sometimes I wonder if we make deals with God in some previous life about what we'll end up with in the next."

Grey rolled over and looked at her. "You sound like a hippie," he said. He picked up the bottle of cabernet and pulled the cork out with his teeth and filled their glasses. Gentle waves smacked slackly against the hull. "I do wonder though."

"What?" she asked.

"How I found you."

She scooted closer and kissed him.

"What happens next?" he said.

"Does it matter?"

"It just feels like something is missing."

"Something is always missing in this world. That's why we don't stay forever."

"We're built to move," he said.

"And so we build things to move us."

"Faster and farther away. We're always chasing something."

"Or running from something."

"But where does it end?"

"You never know," she said. "That's what makes it exciting."

"And terrifying."

"Is there a difference?"

They sipped their wine and rolled onto their backs again to watch the stars.

"Do you think they'll ever find us here?" Grey asked.

"I think we'll be gone first."

"You want to leave?"

"No," she said. "But we will."

"I can't help but think about how it will end. These last few months it hasn't felt real, you know?"

"Has it ever? We only know what we've been told, but we haven't seen anything. It's hard to believe any of it. We haven't seen anyone chasing us. We never saw Mancini's body."

"Yeah."

"Right?" she asked. "You never saw his body."

He looked at her, then he looked away. "Right," he said.

More weeks passed and Misty's suspicions grew, but she said nothing. She watched Grey with the same adoration with which she had always watched him, never pulling him from the pedestal upon which she had placed him, though he seemed less balanced. Whether his unease was rooted in his own guilt or that of his father or simply the unfamiliar uncertainty of course, she did not know. What she did know was that none of it made her question her love for him. She awoke most mornings before him and lay beside him and watched him sleep, listening to his steady breath ebbing and flowing with the tide in the darkness. By sunrise they were swimming in the bay, grabbing at angelfish with their bare hands and never quite catching them. They chased crabs on the beach and cracked coconuts on the rocks and sipped the water from within. They ate and drank and ran in the jungle and they were always together.

Wherever they were, the *Mistical Reflection* maintained her omnipresence, anchored in the bay, the centerpiece of their green and blue panorama. With each day they loved her more, whether they were sailing with her, sleeping upon her, or watching her from the shore. And with each day they also knew the time would soon come when they would board her for yet another journey. To where this time they could not know, but they could not hide forever, nor did they want to. Though perhaps sometimes only subconsciously, they were always watching for their hunters, always eyeing their surroundings for the quickest escape the way prey in the wild hones its instincts for evasion. Their paradise was never quite so. Peace within could never be realized under such dire circumstances, even in the most beautiful of places.

Winter had turned to spring back home, but the weather on Tortola changed little. The nightly calls with Declan were always brief. Grey and Misty awaited direction, but none came. "Just keep waiting," he would say. Always they were waiting, until one clear night as they lay upon the yacht's deck, the instructions changed.

"It's time," said Declan.

"Time for what?" asked Grey.

"You'll need to move back into US territory. The feds can't operate so broadly in the British Virgin Islands."

"Isn't that a good thing?"

"Not anymore. Other players are getting close. We need the help of the FBI now."

"I didn't know you had spoken with McGuinness."

"I haven't."

"What changed then? Why are they on our side now?"

"Nothing has changed," said Declan. "They aren't on your side."

"This doesn't make sense."

"Agents McGuinness and Richter—we're going to let them find you. Then we're going to draw out the other side and create a confrontation."

"By confrontation you mean what, exactly?"

"That depends. But, Grey—"

"Yes?"

"Keep the gun loaded. Remember everything I taught you when you were a kid. I know it's been a long time, but you have more training than most professionals in this game. Use it. Trust your instincts. Watch your surroundings, and whatever you do, do not let them catch you."

Grey closed his eyes. "My name is tarnished forever," he said.

"Your legacy is in your work, not in your name," replied Declan. "Tomorrow morning, gather whatever you need and sail west toward St. Thomas. Rent a slip in Charlotte Amalie, and this time use the credit cards. Don't bother being inconspicuous. Act like you did in the Bahamas—like carefree tourists. We'll talk soon."

The call ended. A flock of seagulls squawked in the night as they flew invisibly overhead. The tide crashed white onto the black beach, candles glowing in the windows of the little house behind it.

"Well, what did he say?" asked Misty.

"We leave tomorrow," said Grey.

"That's it?"

"That's it."

They lay awake through the night, and at sunrise they rose and swam ashore. They skipped breakfast and took the Jeep toward Road Town, bumping up the narrow path into the jungle hills. Grey peered over the cliff just to his left into the empty space that would consume them if just one rock slipped beneath the tires. Then he looked at Misty to his right as the wind blew in her still wet hair, and he took a breath of her sweet fragrance. They wound through the woods and broke back into the sunlight at the edge of town, rolling cautiously through the streets between pastel-colored buildings with hurricane shutters and a few early-rising locals. The tires scraped to a stop in the gravel parking lot where a brood of chickens cackled and scattered chaotically in front of the market that had just opened. They gathered produce and fresh poultry and liquor and quickly left again, headed back to the bay. With their kayaks loaded they paddled out to the yacht. The house and the Jeep were left just as they had been found four months before, and Grey and Misty were once again in the wind, westbound for the US Virgin Islands.

# 21

# Urban Warfare

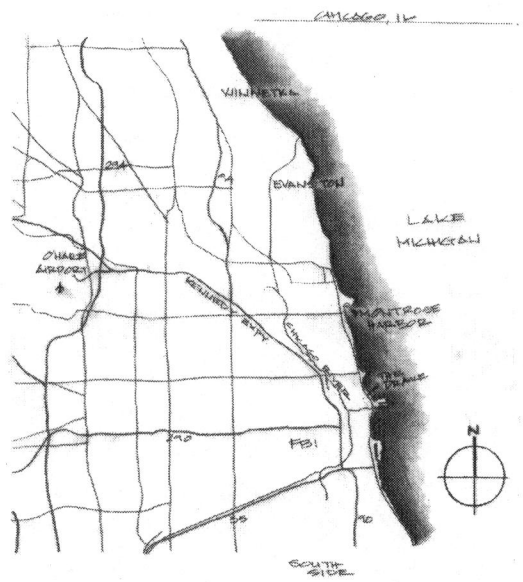

The shot rang in Francesco De Luca's ears as the pink mist appeared in his scope and his target dropped. More shots followed from the South Side street down below, popping distantly as henchmen from both the Mancini and Zanetti mobs opened fire into one another, both believing the other side had fired first. Brick buildings lit up in flashes like lightning in the night. A car exploded and lay burning in the street. In the distance he heard sirens from two—three—five directions and varying distances, all converging upon the scene of carnage he had created. Red and blue lights flashed as they drew near and the shooters still left standing scrambled into a car, tires squealing as they fled.

De Luca's gloved hands were steady as he disassembled his rifle and placed each component snugly into the case. In less than a minute the firefight was over, but the consequences would be momentous and enduring. There was no question; a war had begun. He picked up his brass and put it in his pocket and left the dark and vacant apartment, closing the door behind him. On the staircase a woman ran past him screaming, but he pulled the hood over his head and did not look at her. By the time police arrived on the scene he had vanished leaving no trace behind.

Three blocks away he climbed into the junk car he had purchased in cash earlier in the day and headed toward South Halsted Street then turned north. He dumped the car at a scrap yard by the Chicago River and moved to the jon boat there waiting for him. As the city slept he motored toward downtown against the current, beneath bridges, past the train yard, barreling in the direction of the Willis Tower dead ahead. The buildings grew taller and the night mist glowed yellow under their light. At the fork he turned east to follow alongside Wacker Drive. Beneath DuSable Bridge he pulled to the south side of the river and climbed over the railing onto the empty Chicago Riverwalk and let the boat float away. He looked around from the shadows. He saw no one, and no one had seen him. Casually he took the stairs to the surface and walked north on Michigan Avenue with his rifle inconspicuously packed in the case on his back. Traffic was light. A group of drunken college students stumbled toward him on the sidewalk, obnoxiously rambling as he kept his head down and walked through them, and they barely noticed him. He walked the length of the Magnificent Mile and reached The Drake Hotel where he passed the reception desk quietly and took the elevator to his floor and slipped into his room. There he changed from his black hood and pants and boots into his nightclothes, pulled back the sheets, turned out the lights, and went to sleep.

By the time the sun had risen Francesco De Luca was wide-awake. Lake Michigan sparkled outside his window, and he looked north up Lake Shore Drive. The city had not changed for most, but the single shot fired from his gun in the night had set in motion a dangerous but necessary turning of the table that held so many intertwining fates. The first step of his elaborate plan was complete. Gianni Zanetti and the Mancini mob were gunning for each other, and the FBI could not ignore an all out war in the streets of Chicago.

He shaved and dressed in an Italian-made suit and tie and went to the lobby and stepped outside into the crisp spring morning air. He walked five blocks south on Michigan Avenue, past Water Tower Place on the Magnificent Mile with its shoppers and tourists and business people in suits and turned west on Chicago Avenue and walked three more blocks. At State Street he took the stairs down to the Red Line L station beneath the surface and bought a CTA pass with cash. He stood on the platform awaiting the northbound train beside a police officer who glanced at him, then back at the tracks. When the train arrived and the doors opened, De Luca stepped on and the police officer followed. They stood in the aisle holding the overhead bar and the train sped off, wheels screaming as it leaned around turns and whipped through the still air in the darkness underground, stopping seconds at Clark & Division, then North & Clybourn. It emerged from its subterranean rumble and the sunlight broke through the windows. Cars passed beneath the elevated tracks and pedestrians walked the streets unaware of his existence. At the Fullerton stop the officer stepped off and De Luca remained. Then at Belmont he moved to the northbound Purple Line train.

Sheridan
Wilson
Howard
South Boulevard
Main
Dempster

He stepped off the train at Davis in the heart of downtown Evanston and moved to the UP-N line. He purchased another pass in cash and boarded the next train, continuing north.

Central Street

Wilmette

Kenilworth

Indian Hill

At Winnetka he disembarked. He walked east to a neighborhood of large estates near the shore. The street was quiet. A dog ran across a yard barking at him. He turned and looked it in the eye, and the dog stopped and sat silently and watched him pass. Ahead was a tall iron fence with bold brick columns where two suited men stood guard at a gate in front of a brick mansion mostly hidden by immense trees and foliage. Both put their hands in their jackets as De Luca approached, but his pace did not slow. He stopped in front of them.

"I'm here to see Mr. Zanetti," he said.

"And you are?"

"A former associate of the Mancini family."

The guards stiffened their stances and De Luca heard the subtle clicks of safeties being switched off within their jackets.

"What is your name?" asked one of the guards coarsely.

"Francesco De Luca."

"You don't look Italian, Mr. De Luca."

"Half Italian," he replied. "The better half."

"What is your business with Mr. Zanetti?"

"I have information."

"What sort of information?"

"The sort that I will only discuss with Mr. Zanetti."

The guards looked at each other. One of them stepped away to make a phone call and the other remained with De Luca, staring at him. A moment later the iron gate began to open and the first guard returned.

"Come with me," he said.

The three walked through the gate and it closed behind them. They followed the brick driveway to the porte-cochère at the side of the mansion where the hedges concealed them from the street and neighboring residences, and a black Maybach pulled out of the garage and stopped in front of them. One guard drew his gun and pointed it at De Luca while the other frisked him. When he was satisfied he opened the rear door and De Luca climbed in. The door was closed behind him and the first guard got into the car on the other side as the second moved to the front passenger seat. The guard beside him put a gun to his head.

"Now you'll tell us what information you have to share. We'll pass it on to Mr. Zanetti."

De Luca looked around. "This is a nice car," he said.

"Tell us what you know."

"No."

"No?"

"I told you I'll only talk with Mr. Zanetti."

"You'd rather I kill you right here?"

"You're not going to shoot me," said De Luca.

"Why is that?"

"If you had any intention of killing me you wouldn't be holding a gun to my head in a two hundred thousand dollar car. It's fine, I'll wait."

He closed his eyes and pressed the button to recline his seat. A moment later he heard the creak of the iron gate and felt the car begin to roll. He felt the pavement change from brick to concrete slabs, then asphalt. He felt when they turned onto Sheridan Road, moving southbound and crossing the bridge at Wilmette Harbor. At Isabella Street they turned left where it changed names to Sheridan Road and continued on, veering right again and passing through Northwestern University.

Left at Burnham Place.

Right again on Sheridan Road.

Left again onto South Boulevard.

Veering right as it turned once more to Sheridan Road with the lake just to his left, always knowing of their location by the feel of the road, the turns, the stop signs, the sounds of traffic.

Past Loyola Beach and under the Red Line L station.

Left onto West Hollywood Avenue.

Veering right again at Edgewater Beach, increasing speed.

They exited North Lake Shore Drive in Uptown and turned east toward the lake, stopping at Montrose Harbor. De Luca opened his eyes.

"Let's go," said the guard.

Zanetti's two henchmen got out of the car with De Luca and walked to the harbor and out to the end of a dock where they boarded a speedboat. As it backed out of the slip he watched the car drive off. They pulled out of the harbor and then sped southeast on the blue lake toward Gianni Zanetti's yacht in the distance where he was still holed up. The speedboat came alongside and two henchmen tossed ropes and pulled them in. De Luca boarded the yacht where he was escorted with a firm politeness to the rear of the cabin as the small boat turned away and headed back toward the Chicago skyline. The cabin door was opened and Gianni Zanetti stood from his chair inside.

"Come in, Mr. De Luca."

He stepped inside, followed by a guard who closed the door behind them.

"No, no," said Zanetti, "leave it open. It's a beautiful day. And you can leave our paisan alone here with me. You're not dangerous, are you, Mr. De Luca?"

"That depends on who you are."

Zanetti laughed. "I think we're good here. Thank you, Marco," he said, gesturing to his henchman who reluctantly turned and went back outside. "Now, first things first. Would you like a drink, Mr. De Luca?"

"It's a little early for me, sir."

Zanetti ignored him and walked to the bar and pulled a bottle of Johnnie Walker Blue Label from his cooler. "I recognized your name," he said, setting two glasses on the countertop and pouring each three fingers deep. "One might call you infamous, Mr. De Luca. Three of my men were killed last night. You wouldn't know anything about that, would you?"

"Urban warfare isn't my specialty."

Zanetti took the glasses and walked back around the bar and handed one to De Luca. "Someone has been taking out my people—quietly, one by one, until last night. It's not so quiet anymore."

"The Mancini family blames you for Salvatore's murder. They're coming after you."

"Tell me something I don't know. Why do you think I'm living on this boat?"

"I think I can help you," said De Luca.

"Well, I'm inclined to believe just about anyone right now. I'm getting sick of this boat. I don't even like the water. Whoever this assassin is, he's very effective, and my people can't trace him. And now we have this incident. Street fights like the one last night are messy. The media spotlight is bad for business, and on top of it we have these idealistic new age cops who won't go away. I miss the old days when you could stick a wad of cash in their hands and all the questions stopped. You know what I mean. You're a former employee of the Mancini family."

"Private contractor, actually. Long ago."

"Right. You left Salvatore shortly before his arrest, correct?"

"That's right."

"Interesting timing. You didn't have anything to do with that, did you?" asked Zanetti, eyeing him closely.

"No, sir," said De Luca, taking a sip of his scotch and staring straight back.

"Of course not. It was a silly question."

"My job had been completed, and I moved on."

"Well, it's none of my business. Either way, it created an opportunity for me to expand. So you have no loyalty to the Mancinis? These shootings of my people, well, you must imagine it makes me a little suspicious of strangers like yourself—particularly strangers with your reputation."

"That's not how I work," said De Luca. "I don't waste my time with low-level thugs, and this war is just as messy for the Mancinis. With all due respect, if I had been hired to take care of you, you'd never have the chance to be suspicious. My loyalty is to the highest bidder. I go where I'm needed, and you need my help."

"Is that so?" said Zanetti, raising his eyebrows. "Then tell me, Mr. De Luca, what *is* your specialty?"

"Hunting."

"Hunting," Zanetti repeated with a nod. "And who might we be talking about?"

"Grey Cavanaugh."

"Ah, Grey Cavanaugh. I have that handled."

"Do you? I understand your people haven't been able to locate him for four months."

"He has been unexpectedly evasive, I'll admit, but I have a man inside the investigation."

"Whoever he is, I'm not so sure I'd trust him," said De Luca. "So far he's been sloppy at best, duplicitous at worst, and you need this to be clean and quick. You know the FBI is tracking both your people and Mancini's. If it looks like Grey Cavanaugh was murdered then both the feds and the Mancinis will think you're tying up loose ends. Of course, it's not likely that the feds could actually charge you for a distant murder, but the Mancini family doesn't need proof to come after you. They must believe Cavanaugh acted alone. The evidence of his guilt is already there. Now we just need to keep your fingerprints off of his demise."

"What do you propose?"

"Put me on the hunt. And don't tell any of your people."

Gianni Zanetti looked out the window at the city beyond the blue. Then he slowly sat down in his armchair with De Luca standing over him and took the last swig from his glass. "Alright," he said.

"You're making the right decision," said De Luca. "Now, first, I need to know who you have on the inside."

The phone rang and Zanetti answered. He sat listening as De Luca looked down upon the vacant dome of his head, waiting. Wrinkles formed on the boss's brow as the indistinguishable words of the voice on the other end came through severe and abrasive and his cheeks flushed and he began to sweat. A minute later he set the phone aside and looked up.

"Well, Mr. De Luca," he said, "that was my man on the inside, and it seems we've found Grey Cavanaugh. There's been a shootout in the Virgin Islands."

# 22

# Trouble in Paradise

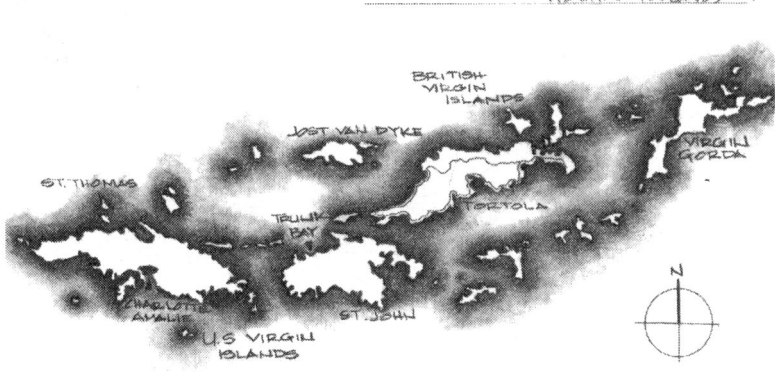

The sun rose over Charlotte Amalie on the third morning after their arrival in St. Thomas. Grey and Misty watched from the deck of the *Mistical Reflection* as the orange glow peeked over the tropical hills and black shadows turned to vivid green. Steam rose from their coffee mugs in the still morning air. A cruise ship slowly idled into the bay between Hassel Island and Havensight Point and coasted to a stop at the West Indian Company Dock where thousands of vacationers would soon disembark and disperse into the streets, blissfully unaware of the dangerous turn their morning would soon take. Unbeknownst to Grey and Misty, at that same moment two planes approached the island—one a passenger airliner carrying agents McGuinness and Richter, the other a private jet where five of Zanetti's henchmen were loading their weapons.

The harbor grew busy with people boarding catamarans departing for sightseeing and snorkeling tours as Grey and Misty left their yacht tied up to the pier and walked the brick-lined boardwalk toward town. Stucco buildings and palm trees shaded the roadways. Crowds of shoppers flooded the sidewalks as doors opened, anxious to spend their money on expensive duty-free merchandise.

It was unusually hot for May, nearly ninety degrees by mid-morning with humidity that signaled an imminent storm and drove sweaty pedestrians with cameras and shopping bags into the air-conditioned storefronts lining the streets. Gray clouds rolled in the distance trailing a soft cape of precipitation. Misty stood gazing between the buildings toward the bay.

"It's going to rain," said Grey.

"I know," she smiled. "It's beautiful."

"We should go inside."

"I'd rather stay out here."

"You want to spend the rest of the day soaking wet?"

"Life's full of regrets," she said. "What's one more?"

Soon the rain was upon them. The sky dimmed and thunder rumbled as Grey and Misty ran through the puddles laughing. She spun in circles, looking up to the sky with her mouth open and arms outstretched, and he watched her, as free a spirit as there could be, drinking the rain as it poured down. They moved beneath an awning and she wrapped her arms around him and they held each other close.

"I love you," he said.

"I love you more."

She squeezed him tighter for a moment and then stepped back and looked through the rain into the window of an art gallery across the street, then back at Grey.

"Your dad did say to spend freely, right?"

"He did."

"Something to bring home?" she suggested. "A souvenir?"

"I had something else in mind," he said.

"Yeah? Like what?"

"Can't tell you."

"Why not?" she pouted.

"It would ruin the surprise. Let's meet back here in, say, two hours?"

"Grey, I don't know if splitting up is a good idea right now."

"It's just a couple of hours, and this is such a public place. Nobody would dare try anything out here in the middle of the day."

"If you say so."

He leaned in and put his lips to her ear. "But if it makes you feel better," he whispered, "the gun is in your purse."

She looked up at him to speak, but before she could object he silenced her with a kiss. Reluctantly, she turned away and walked across the street. On the other side she turned again and looked at him through the traffic and wrung her hair out on the sidewalk and tied it up dripping onto the back of her neck, and she waved to him before walking inside.

They had spent nearly every moment together for so many months that it was strange to be apart, particularly in such a public venue. As he walked down the street he looked back at the gallery windows where Misty mixed with the other faces. With the gun at her side he was certain that she was safer than he was, and that was the way he preferred it, but even he felt safe in the crowd. Nothing he saw suggested that either of them were in any sort of danger.

Blocks away, he stepped into a jewelry store where diamonds and precious metals sparkled in an array of brilliant colors under the white lights projected upon them within their rich wood and crystal showcases. The ambiance was otherwise dim and quiet. Grey moved slowly around the perimeter, gazing through the glass at watches and necklaces and bracelets without price tags, and he paused at the case of engagement rings. He leaned over the countertop and peered in, closely examining the selection of unique designs and diamonds of varying size and color and clarity. One in particular caught his eye.

The hand of a man in a black suit and brass cufflinks extended over the glass holding a white towel embroidered with the image of a diamond.

"It's a wet one out there," he said.

"It is," replied Grey, taking the towel and drying his face and hands. "Thank you."

"Of course, sir. Now, you're in the market for an engagement ring?"

"I am."

"Well, congratulations. Where are you from?"

"Chicago," said Grey, careful not to divulge any information that might lead to discovery of his true identity.

"I see," said the jeweler. "Dangerous place these days, I hear."

"Oh yeah?"

"According to the news. They haven't caught that killer yet, have they?"

"Forgive me," said Grey, "I don't pay much attention to the news."

"I'm surprised you could avoid it. They say there's a mysterious sniper in Chicago picking people off in the streets. Last I heard the police had no suspects. He leaves no trace. But they say his victims all seem to have mafia ties, so perhaps you're safe. Assuming you're not involved in organized crime," he laughed.

Grey turned nervously and looked across the warm and dim shop at the bright white glowing entrance with its hurricane doors standing open and the rain still pouring down outside.

"No matter," the jeweler went on, "you're on vacation, and you're in love. Love conquers all, right? So, tell me what you're looking for."

They spoke for over an hour as the jeweler presented Grey with dozens of rings, all beautiful and distinctive, but he always gravitated back to the one that had first drawn him in. It was perfect, he thought—not extravagant or opulent, but elegant and understated, just as was the yacht he had designed for the love of his life. As he looked upon it in the palm of his hand though, he wondered just how long Misty would be able to sustain this life before he was no longer worth the sacrifice. He wondered whether the ring would solidify that bond or drive her to wish for what they had lost. He wondered if he would be better off waiting before asking her to make any further commitments to him, and he circled the store once more, mulling over his decision before stepping back out into the storm.

The time was nearing for their rendezvous beneath the canopy where he had left her, but Grey had only just begun the walk back when he felt the barrel of a gun on his spine.

"Keep walking," said the unfamiliar voice behind him.

His hands trembled as a rush of adrenaline pulsed through his veins, and suddenly it was all real. That supposed threat from which they had been on the run for over half a year was in that moment no longer hypothetical, and immediately he thought of Misty. She would not go without a fight, he knew, and he had heard no gunshots.

There was no panic in the streets. He knew they had found him first.

"Where are we going?"

"There's a car waiting at the next corner. Let's make this quiet and your girlfriend won't be hurt."

Grey was unconvinced. As the car pulled up and the rear door opened from the inside he turned and grabbed the hand holding the gun and pointed it to the sky. The gun went off and chaos erupted at the intersection. Approaching vehicles skidded to a stop and pedestrians ran screaming in all directions. Grey threw his attacker into the rear seat of the car, knocking back the man inside, and took off running down an alley. Gunshots popped behind him and stucco shattered from the walls on either side as he narrowly escaped each slug. He rounded the next corner, slipping on the wet pavement and smacking the ground as a bullet whizzed past his ear and shattered a window across the street, and he was up again in an instant, sprinting with his head down to minimize the target.

In the distance he saw Misty standing where he had left her two hours before. She looked up and froze at the bedlam that followed him as he came racing toward her down the street.

"Misty, run!" he yelled.

She turned and ducked around the next corner as he ran to catch up, his lungs burning with each heavy breath and the rain blurring his vision. In the harbor beyond he could see the *Mistical Reflection*, but even if they could reach her there was no chance of making it out of the harbor quickly enough for an escape, even under power. They would need an alternative.

Nearby there was a row of speedboats for rent. With a powerful engine they could quickly flee to St. John and hide out in the island's expansive national park, but before he could yell ahead to Misty he was tackled to the ground. The attacker struck him in the face and he swung back, missing once, then connecting with the next. The man fell back dazed, and a second came down upon Grey with punch after punch to the gut and began to drag him limp into an alley, and through it all he feared only that Misty was next. He knew she would not leave him alone, and her love for him could very well get her killed.

He fought back for both of their lives, but as Zanetti's men beat him in the street under the pouring rain his chances for survival dimmed. He wondered why they did not simply shoot him if they wanted him dead, and just as the thought came and went he was looking down the barrel of a gun. He closed his eyes, and then he heard the shot. The pressure of crushing blows stopped and the pain faded as he began to lose consciousness. It seemed like minutes had passed before he opened his eyes again and another shot came with a flash that lit up the sky. Then he saw smoke pouring from the barrel of the gun in Misty's hand as she came running toward him. Two more shots went off before she reached him.

"Get up, Grey!"

He groaned, climbing to his feet as the two henchmen who had reached him first rolled bloody on the ground and their car came sliding around the corner.

"We have to go!" Misty screamed, aiming the gun and letting off another shot into the windshield. She took his hand and pulled him toward the harbor where the *Mistical Reflection* waited. He struggled to redirect her, but he was weakened and could not speak. He only hoped there were enough rounds left in the gun to hold off the few remaining gangsters. As they drew near the yacht there were two men walking toward them on the boardwalk, their eerie silhouettes growing in the gray mist over the bay, and drawing near those two faces took familiar forms. Grey and Misty froze in their tracks, as did Agents McGuinness and Richter looking back at them.

Before any of them could speak they were bombarded with a fusillade of gunshots from the shore. Grey and Misty dropped to the ground as the agents drew their guns and took cover behind bollards on opposite sides of the pier.

"Get out of the way!" yelled McGuinness, aiming around them and firing back. Grey and Misty crawled on the ground to keep out of the line of fire. Visible streaks appeared in the air as bullets cut through raindrops over the boardwalk. Richter remained crouched behind the bollard, splintering with each round that struck. He watched with furious frustration as the target he had been chasing for so many months inched his way between him and his colleague.

"Take cover!" McGuinness yelled again, his voice in competition with roaring gunshots just as Grey and Misty came alongside the *Mistical Reflection*. They rolled from the pier over the gunwale and onto the yacht's deck and hastily untied the ropes from the cleats. Grey lay there panting, barely conscious as Misty started the engine and threw it in reverse. The hull scraped the side of the pier and bounced off of another boat anchored nearby. The chaos shrunk as she turned the wheel and came about in the harbor and flung the transmission into forward, heading out toward the open ocean. She looked back at the faint flashes of gunfire beyond their wake and at Richter's face as he glared straight back across the bay, watching as they escaped once again.

# 23

## A Ghost Arisen

"Don't just sit there!" yelled McGuinness. "Shoot!" Richter closed his eyes and shook his head as the rage washed over him, and he stood from behind the bollard and pointed his gun and pulled the trigger over and over again, firing erratically back at Zanetti's men.

"Hey! Who the hell taught you to fire a gun?" said McGuinness. "You're going to hit a civilian like that!"

The slide on Richter's pistol locked back as he emptied the magazine, and he dropped back down behind the post to reload.

"You told me to shoot," he said. "I'm holding them off."

"Try aiming," McGuinness replied as he peered around his shelter. "I'm almost out of rounds."

"How many are there?"

"I see three shooters. Two more on the ground. Looks like they've been hit."

Richter loaded his spare magazine and chambered a round. He took aim around the bollard and fired off a quick succession of shots until the trigger clicked, but all three shooters remained standing. McGuinness looked at him for a moment and then pointed his own weapon and sighted in his target. He fired his last few rounds. One of Zanetti's henchmen fell.

"Well, what now?" asked Richter.

McGuinness looked around.

"Where the hell are the cops?"

"Probably paid to stay away."

The sound of squealing tires interrupted them, and McGuinness looked toward the shore. A car came drifting around a corner, barreling toward the two remaining shooters. Before they could react, both were pulled beneath the tires and dragged half a block where the car skidded to a stop. The sounds of gunshots ceased, replaced by the rumble of thunder and screaming bystanders.

McGuinness and Richter jumped from their cover and ran the boardwalk toward the street. There they found the two crushed shooters and the one McGuinness had shot all dead. The other two were still on the sidewalk wailing in agony from the bullets Misty had fired. The driver stepped out of the car and over the bodies.

"Are you alright?" asked McGuinness.

"Better than these guys," said the driver.

"What's your name?"

"Tobias."

"Alright, Tobias," he said as a parade of police SUVs approached through the gathering crowd. "Hang out here after you're done with the police. We'll need to talk to you as well."

He held up his badge as police officers rushed the scene and began taping it off.

"I need to make a call," said Richter, stepping away.

"Yeah," said McGuinness, taking out his own phone just as it began to ring. "The office is calling."

He answered the call, looking out to the horizon where the *Mistical Reflection* had disappeared.

"Conrad."

"Carla."

"You guys need to get back here. We have a mess in Chicago."

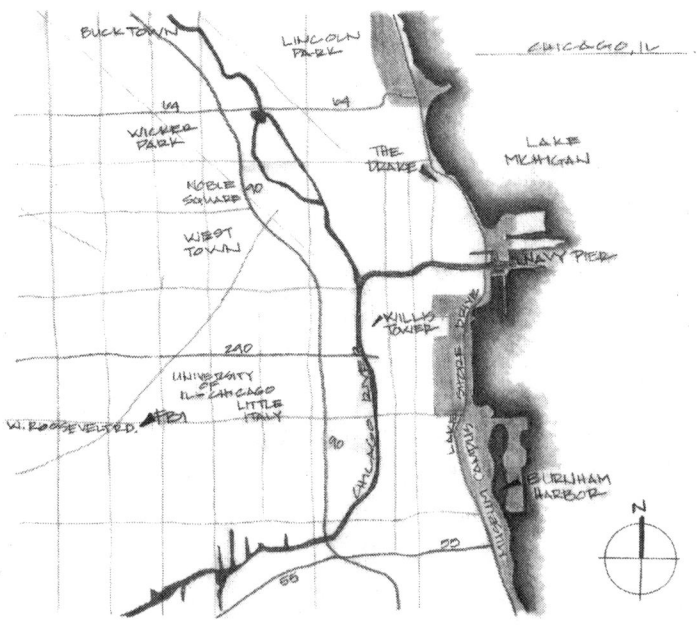

That evening their plane touched down at O'Hare where both agents twitched anxiously as they sat on the tarmac, waiting for their turn to taxi up to the gate. They peered out the window into the night, a glow hovering over the city outside. When they finally reached the gate the flight attendants instructed the passengers to remain in their seats as the hatch opened and the two agents briskly exited ahead of the rest. An FBI escort was waiting to take them to the scene of the shootout on the South Side the night before. McGuinness smiled as they emerged from the jet bridge and his eyes fell upon an old friend.

"Well, well, well, Special Agent Carla Sanborn. It's been a long time."

"Too long," she said. "We've missed you in Chicago."

"Wish I could say the same—about Chicago I mean. Of course I've missed you, Carla."

"It's good to see you, Conrad. I heard you had some excitement this morning."

"You could say that. Three dead, two in custody, all low-level Zanetti thugs. Unfortunately, the guy who saved our lives disappeared before anyone had a chance to talk to him. It makes me wonder if he—I don't know—knew just where to be. We haven't gotten anything out of the two guys we arrested, but it's clear they were after our suspect in the Mancini murder. How they found him down there I have no idea. I don't imagine they got the same anonymous call that we did."

"The mob hasn't gotten this kind of attention since—well—Mancini's trial," she said. "This scale of violence, it's like they forgot what decade they're in. Two shootouts on the same morning two thousand miles apart, both involving Gianni Zanetti. Coincidence?"

"Not likely," replied McGuinness. "He's really going out of his way."

"There are rumors around here that he's gone into business with Los Zetas. If they're true that would explain a lot. We've been scraping the scene on the South Side all day. You want to wait until tomorrow to check it out?"

"You know me better than that, Carla. Where's your car?"

The three agents headed east from the airport on the Kennedy Expressway.

Through Norwood Park.

Southeast through Jefferson Park.

Irving Park.

Avondale.

Bucktown,

South through Noble Square.

McGuinness scanned the maze of onramps and offramps and overpasses outside, catching glimpses of the skyline between buildings and breaks in sound walls. The city was just a little bit different than when he had left it. They crossed the empty black south branch of the Chicago River, the ripples of its subtle current twinkling under the stars. They exited the highway on the South Side and rolled discreetly up to the bloody block lit up like day under the police floodlights on telescopic masts overhead.

Agent Sanborn parked the black Suburban in the middle of the street at the crime scene tape and the three agents exited the vehicle. They flashed their credentials to a Chicago Police officer standing guard and he let them pass. A burned out Lincoln Navigator riddled with bullet holes sat upon a wet patch of pavement where the fire department had hosed it down. Beside it, chalk outlines indicated where two men had taken their last breaths.

"How many dead?" asked Richter.

"Five," said Sanborn. "Two of Mancini's guys crashed a few blocks away as they were fleeing the scene, DOA. Three of Zanetti's here. One of them was in the Navigator there. It doesn't look like anyone involved made it out alive."

McGuinness walked alone to the other end of the block, maneuvering around police officers and forensic analysts, quietly examining the scene, reconstructing it in his mind. The positions of the bodies. Tire tracks of the escaping vehicle. The locations of bullet holes marked on the pavement and surrounding brick walls. Broken windows in the buildings. He paced the street as Carla Sanborn watched him, always fascinated by the way he seemed to visualize the entirety of such a complex event. She missed watching him work. They were both better when they worked together, she knew, but she understood why he had to leave Chicago. His time undercover had taken its toll, and the move was his last futile effort to save his second marriage. She wondered if part of that meant getting away from her.

She could see his vexation as he made his way back toward them, looking around, seeking the impetus that had led to the carnage. It didn't add up. Both the Mancinis and Zanettis were ruthless, but in his experience neither was so sloppy as to engage in such brazen urban warfare in their own city. Then she saw his eyes widen. He turned, walking across the chalk outline of one of the fallen shooters, crossed the sidewalk, and knelt at the base of the wall of an adjacent building. Agents Sanborn and Richter followed.

"This hole isn't tagged," said McGuinness, shining a flashlight into it. "Carla, what were these guys shooting?"

"These three here had nine millimeters, and we found two forty cals in the car that crashed."

"That's not what made this hole. Look at the diameter, and it's far too deep."

Agent Sanborn called over the forensics team. "We need to extract this slug and check the angle," she said.

As the agents watched, the gloved investigators delicately pulled the chunk of metal out of the wall and placed it in an evidence bag for ballistics testing. They slipped a trajectory rod into the vacant hole and screwed a laser onto the protruding end. "Lights," yelled Agent Sanborn, and one by one the floodlights were powered down, darkening the block until the only light left was the green laser projected from the bullet hole. All eyes followed its line cutting through the thin night mist to where it ended at the window of an abandoned building down the block and across the street.

"Well," said McGuinness, "it looks like we have a sixth shooter."

The three agents stood under the white ambient light of the forensics lab awaiting the arrival of the analyst. McGuinness rubbed his eyes, weary from travel and two days without sleep. Once he had finally reached the hotel he had spent the remainder of the night reviewing investigation reports, closely examining the crime scene photos and witness accounts. Aside from the bullet hole that only he had noticed and the massive entry and exit wounds in the torso of one of Zanetti's men, there was not a shred of evidence suggesting that anyone other than the five dead mobsters had fired shots. The abandoned building from where the shot had come was clean.

The lab analyst came into the room with a manila folder in his hand. "We have good news and bad news," he said. "The good news is that we've identified the mystery weapon. It's a Kivaari three thirty-eight Lapua Magnum, a specialty takedown sniper rifle that can be disassembled in seconds and carried in a suitcase or backpack. This appears to be the sixth of Gianni Zanetti's men killed by this gun in the last few months, all single shots to the chest. Zanetti must have really pissed somebody off."

"And the bad news?" asked Sanborn.

"Well, it'll take a while to comb through the rest of the evidence collected, but I don't expect we'll turn up anything on the sniper. He's left us nothing to go on at any of the scenes. This guy is a ghost."

McGuinness shook his head. "I'm not surprised," he said. "Well, we know this was the first shot fired; this victim still had his gun holstered. The rest pulled theirs after he was hit."

"This guy's really gunning for Zanetti," said Sanborn.

"I'm not so sure," replied McGuinness.

"What do you mean?"

"This mess was totally unnecessary if he was just going after Zanetti. I don't think he's working for the Mancini family. I think he's working for someone else—or worse, he's working alone. He's starting a war."

"I don't buy it," said Richter. "Salvatore Mancini was murdered. The Mancini family obviously thinks Zanetti did it, so they're retaliating."

"Then what about Grey Cavanaugh?"

"He's the guy who *really* did it, of course."

"You don't actually think it's that simple, do you, Robert?"

"Why not?"

"I'm with Conrad on this," said Agent Sanborn. "This situation just keeps getting more complicated. Accusing an architect with a clean record of murdering a mob boss is strange enough to begin with, but now that architect has managed to drop off the grid and evade you guys for months, and on top of it we have a gruesome mob war and a rogue sniper. And if Grey Cavanaugh did kill Mancini and he acted alone, why is Zanetti sending men to chase him down thousands of miles away? Why would he care?"

Richter shrugged.

"Only one way to find out," said McGuinness. "Let's go have a chat with Gianni Zanetti."

Agent Sanborn smiled.

"This ought to be interesting."

They stepped out of the building, walking toward the visitor parking lot on West Roosevelt Road. The returning lunch crowd passed by them on the sidewalk and a man on his phone bumped into McGuinness and kept walking. With all this technology, he thought, the job sure has changed, and people have lost their manners. Retirement was looking better every day. The three agents climbed into Sanborn's Suburban and pulled out of the lot and onto the road and then turned north on Damen Avenue headed toward Winnetka. McGuinness watched the buildings of Chicago's neighborhoods changing as they passed by, eliciting dueling sentiments of nostalgia and nausea. The last time he had seen Gianni Zanetti was during the first Mancini investigation when Zanetti still thought him a faithful servant of the family, before his cover was revealed and the name Conrad McGuinness became famous among criminal investigators and mafia alike. He wondered how his return would be received. Either way, whether by nostalgic trust or haughty confidence, the Gianni Zanetti he knew would be more likely to answer questions if they came from a familiar face.

The Suburban rolled up to the brick manor on the quiet street and parked in front of the iron gate and its suited guards. McGuinness stepped out onto the curb alone and approached.

"I'd like to speak with Mr. Zanetti."

One guard stepped forward.

"You know better than that, Conrad."

"Do we know each other?"

"Everyone knows who you are, Special Agent McGuinness. Lots of familiar faces coming around lately."

"Yeah? Who else?"

The guard smiled. "Mr. Zanetti is on vacation," he said.

"Vacation, huh? Where?"

"You're the FBI. Figure it out."

McGuinness went back to the Suburban and climbed into the passenger side.

"He's not here."

"You're sure?" asked Sanborn.

"Yes. He would have jumped at the opportunity to see me. But I don't think he went far—not with everything that's going on. He can't afford to look weak. Let's head to Burnham Harbor. It's the only harbor in the city that will accommodate his yacht. He's kept it there for years."

They drove south on Sheridan Road to Lake Shore Drive alongside the great blue lake and its beaches and parks. Sailboats rocked in the harbors as they passed by, rows of matching white hulls shining in the sun, and McGuinness speculated on the whereabouts of Grey Cavanaugh and Misty Sommer. They had been only feet away in St. Thomas, and now he had a new card in his hand—he had seen their vessel. He had seen her beautiful lines and rich wood tones and the name, *Mistical Reflection*, inscribed across her stern, and he knew that such a vessel with her conspicuous elegance had never been designed for evasion. Grey and Misty had never planned on running from anyone.

The FBI vehicle rolled onto the museum campus and parked in the roundabout at the Burnham Harbor office. The three agents walked the length of the harbor and out to the end of Dock C, but Zanetti's yacht was not there. They went to the office where a woman stood from behind the desk. McGuinness set his badge on the counter.

"Are you the harbormaster?"

"Yes, sir."

"Good. We're looking for a yacht."

"Sure," she said, pulling up the harbor registry on the computer. "Whose yacht?"

"Gianni Zanetti's."

"Oh, Mr. Zanetti. I don't even have to look. He took his yacht out last October and hasn't been back all season."

"October? Where did he go?"

"Just out on the lake."

"All winter?" asked McGuinness.

"I guess. Not sure where he went during deep freeze periods, but I still see the yacht out there on occasion."

"They don't come in to refuel?"

"Not here."

"OK, we'll need to have the Coast Guard send a boat for us."

The harbormaster picked up her VHF radio, but before she spoke McGuinness stopped her.

"Not over the radio," he said. "What's the phone number for Station Calumet Harbor?"

He took out his cell phone and dialed as she spoke, *773-768-4093*.

Ten minutes later a Special Purpose Craft idled into the harbor and pulled alongside the walk behind the harbor office. Four well-built Coast Guardsmen came from the cabin and out to the deck. One stepped forward onto the red collar that wrapped the hull.

"We were wondering when you guys might show up," he said, tossing each of the agents a life vest. "Come aboard. Let's go see the man."

"You know the yacht?" asked Richter as they stepped onto the boat.

"Of course. That's a high profile vessel with an even higher profile passenger. We board it regularly for inspections. Needless to say we've never found anything to charge him with, but it's good to make our presence known."

The boat motored slowly out of the harbor. When they reached open water the coxswain hit the throttle and the bow rose into the air, leaping the chop as they accelerated, then leveled out. McGuinness watched as a distant white vessel grew on the horizon and the Chicago skyline shrunk behind them. The yacht floated alone far from the shore due east of the city where its mafia crew could see approaching vessels a long way off. As the Coast Guard craft slowed, three crewmembers snapped magazines into their assault rifles and chambered rounds.

"You guys approach every vessel this way?" asked Richter.

"No, sir," said a crewmember. "Not usually."

They pulled alongside and the coxswain switched on the PA system.

"Gianni Zanetti, this is the US Coast Guard."

"Afternoon, gentlemen," yelled Zanetti, emerging from the cabin between a pair of armed henchmen. He put a hand over his brow and looked at Agent Sanborn. "And lady."

"Hello, Gianni," said McGuinness.

Zanetti froze and his eyes widened. "Could that be my old friend, Aldo Cunetto?" he said, his face glowing with a seemingly genuine expression of joy. He stretched his arms out to his sides. "I'm sorry, Conrad. Old habits. Please, come aboard!"

They tied up and the armed Coast Guard crew boarded the yacht, followed by the agents who kept their weapons holstered.

"Let's talk inside," said Zanetti as he led them into the cabin. "You just missed me too much to stay away from Chicago, right, Conrad?"

"Sure, Gianni."

"I knew it! I know why you're here though. You're here to ask me what I know about that mess on the South Side the other night. Terrible thing. Let me save you the trouble and assure you that I had nothing to do with that. But you already knew that, Conrad. You know I don't operate that way. You were undercover with my organization long enough to know that we use more discretion than that. We really are a family, you know."

"I know that, Gianni," said McGuinness, glancing around the opulent room as they spoke. "We still have to ask."

"I understand."

"It looks like the sniper who's been taking out your people was involved in that shootout," said Agent Sanborn.

Zanetti sighed and shook his head. "I'm not surprised," he said. "Any leads?"

"Not yet."

"Of course not."

"What do you know about the murder of Salvatore Mancini?" she asked.

"Other than what I read in the papers?"

"Yes."

"Well, I know there's no evidence linking me to the crime. I know the Mancinis are claiming that I'm behind it, so they're trying to kill me. And I know it was an inside job."

McGuinness glanced at the bar top beside him and noticed a notepad with the name *De Luca* written along with a phone number. He turned back to Zanetti.

"Is that why your people are chasing down Grey Cavanaugh in the Virgin Islands?"

Zanetti looked to the ceiling and scratched his bald head.

"Grey Cavanaugh, Grey Cavanaugh. Why does that name sound familiar?"

"He's the prime suspect in the Mancini murder."

"Ah, yes. But why would I be after him?"

"Tying up loose ends," Agent Sanborn jumped in.

"Sweetheart," Zanetti laughed, "you make me sound so sinister! I'm just a businessman. I did hear about the trouble in paradise. Ironic that it happened the same day as our unfortunate situation here, but I assure you that if my people were involved I don't know anything about it. I'll look into it, but you really should be focusing your efforts on the Mancinis. Sal's nephew was next in line as head of the family. Seems he took some lessons from his uncle. Ruthless people, the Mancinis. You know that, Conrad. That's why you busted Sal all those years ago and not me. So, you see, you're talking to the wrong Italian."

"Alright," said McGuinness, taking out a business card and setting it on a table. "Thanks for your time, Gianni. Give me a call if you want to talk more."

"Of course. It's good to see you, Conrad. Come and visit any time."

"Sure."

"And tell your friend Richter there to speak up. He looks like he has something to say."

Once they had returned to the harbor, Richter separated to run down Salvatore Mancini's nephew with the Chicago PD while Agents McGuinness and Sanborn headed back to the FBI field office. On the way they stopped for a pizza at Atino's and sat at the bar looking out at the busy intersection of Roosevelt and Jefferson as the sun began to set.

"I miss this pizza," said McGuinness, lifting a thick slice of Chicago-style deep-dish from the pan and onto his plate and cutting the strings of cheese away with his knife.

"Me too," replied Sanborn.

"You work right down the street. We used to come here all the time."

"Yeah. Not anymore."

"No?"

"Like many things, it's not the same without you, Conrad."

He looked at her, then took a bite.

"Listen," he said. "I wanted to talk to you without Richter around."

"Yeah?"

"I saw something on Zanetti's yacht."

"What?"

"A name. Written on a pad of paper. De Luca."

"De Luca?" she repeated. "As in Francesco De Luca? The mob hit man?"

"I think so."

"There's a name from the past. He vanished around the time you busted Mancini, right? We all figured he was murdered," she scoffed. "You think he's back from the dead?"

"That's one way to put it."

"What do you mean?"

McGuinness took another bite and looked around as he chewed.

"Come on," said Sanborn, nudging him.

"I know him. Francesco De Luca."

"What, like personally?" she asked incredulously, setting her fork on the plate.

"Yes. And Francesco De Luca is not his real name."

"Then what is it?"

"His real name is Declan Cavanaugh. He's Grey Cavanaugh's father."

She stared at him speechless as he went on.

"Also, I found this in my pocket earlier," said McGuinness, taking out a note and setting it on the counter where they both read and reread the words.

*Zanetti has a man inside.*

She looked up at him as he folded the note and slipped it back into his pocket.

"Let's keep this between us for now."

# 24

## June

Misty lowered the sails as they coasted into a quiet and deserted bay within Virgin Islands National Park just three hours after the Charlotte Amalie shootout. Beside her Grey lay unconscious, bloody, and bruised, but the deep and labored rising and falling of his chest told her that the fight had not left him. She dropped the anchor and knelt over him, her shadow protecting his face from the sun, and she stroked his cheek gently.

"Grey," she whispered. "I'm here. You're going to be OK."

After a few moments his eyes fluttered open and he coughed in visible agony and spat onto the deck. His saliva was clear, and Misty sighed with relief.

"Where are we?" he asked.

"St. John."

"Did anyone follow us?"

"No," she said. "They were still shooting at each other."

"They're too close. They'll find us within a day."

"I tried your father already. No answer."

Grey closed his eyes. "Why would he send us into a firefight?" he muttered.

"I don't know, but we don't have time to think about that. What do we do now?"

"Ankur left a number," he wheezed. "His satphone. I'm pretty sure the feds don't know about it."

"How is Ankur going to help us?"

"He's been all over the world and he has friends everywhere. Maybe he knows someone on the island. It's our only shot. The number is beside the radio. Use our satphone."

Grey's head fell onto the decking and he lost consciousness.

Misty was still standing over him the next time he awoke. Night had fallen and he could still hear the tide crashing on the beach outside, but he did not feel the rocking of the boat. He opened his eyes and looked around the unfamiliar room. It was small and stark, save for the collections of sailing accessories and spare boat parts. Misty ran her fingers through his hair.

"How are you feeling?" she asked.

"Beaten."

"Well you look better since we cleaned you up."

"We?"

"You were right; Ankur has friends everywhere. Sophie has a small dockyard on the island. She's going to let us stay with her."

"Where's the boat?"

"Covered. Nobody will find us here. Just relax."

Their host scarcely returned to her hillside home, and they spent most of the time during Grey's recovery alone. The thick jungle cloaked the house in green, but through the trees they could see the surf far below, its turquoise clarity turning to heavy sparkling darkness as it stretched to the horizon. They lay by the pool and swam during the day, and at night they left the windows and doors open to the outside. The ubiquitous sounds of waves and wildlife filled their dreams.

Over the weeks Grey's bruises gradually healed. Still they did not try to reach Declan, nor did their satellite phone ring with his incoming call. Both wondered wordlessly where he could be and what kept him silent, and they both hoped that silence was a part of his covert design. They feared the worst, but neither spoke of their fears.

They took Sophie's Jeep into the jungle hills on narrow winding roads where the trees and fronds swayed above them and the sound of tires on wet pavement was the only synthetic thing they heard. Everywhere was bright green except for glimpses of blue horizon and sky through flowing flora. Shadows of clouds crawled across the hills painting their contours in shade and opening up to the sun again. A brief rain came nearly every day, strong and steady with unpredictable timing. Simultaneously, every vehicle would pull to the side of the road as drivers shifted into four-wheel drive to manage the slippery grade and then merge back onto the pavement. The rain would leave as suddenly as it arrived, and again the sky would brighten.

For days they stayed at Trunk Bay. The turquoise surf rolled in gently on the fine white sand, not crashing, but sweeping onto the beach with softness having been subdued by the isles beyond. The green hills of Great Tobago and Jost Van Dyke and the nearer cays formed a comfortable barrier, protecting the bay and Grey and Misty from the great beyond that was always more appealing with a hull beneath their feet. On the land they sought security and shelter, but on the sea there seemed no danger.

They swam out to the small rocky cay within the bay and climbed through its wild vegetation, and they stood in the clearest of water on its north side, invisible to the tourists on the beach behind them. They stood there as a cloud passed over and rain began to fall. The water was still—not like the open ocean or a small pond or anything in between, but like a picture from a dream. A fog floated on its glassy surface disappearing in gray all but the immediate sea, and they looked into it to find themselves looking back. In that fluid mirror they saw a love as deep and complex and full of mystery as the ocean itself. Misty turned to Grey and wrapped herself around him, kissing him deeply, and they made love in the ocean under the pouring rain.

She was always watching him, even when he was not aware, pining for a whisper of the secrets that she had grown certain he kept within. She wondered whether she could ever have known him fully the way she had come to know him had they not been forced to run, and she pondered the perhaps unintended metaphor from the writing of naturalist Henry Beston as he watched the flocks in migration, "that no one really knows a bird until he has seen it in flight." She wondered still why Grey could remember nothing of the events in Chicago, or if he did in fact remember more than he let her know. She wondered about the secrets within the building plans that he claimed to know nothing about. And she wondered if it was possible that Grey did kill Salvatore Mancini.

"Do you like it here?" he asked her.

"It's perfect," she said.

"Yeah."

"Don't you think?"

"On its surface. But even perfection is fleeting. There's always something else to wish for. That's the nature of humanity; we're never satisfied, always wanting more."

"What do you wish for?"

"Freedom," he said. "I miss the open sea. I miss the *Reflection*—her sails, the wind. I hate the thought of her sitting alone in a dockyard garage."

"We'll be back with her soon."

"Not soon enough."

"For most people, the destination is the place where we are right now."

"I'd rather be moving."

"You're always moving," she said. "Don't you want to settle down?"

"I feel free when I'm moving. The yacht is like my baby."

"What about me?"

"I just mean every sailor has a sort of sacred attachment to his vessel, you know? That's why the captain goes down with his ship."

"Grey, that's dark."

"It's the truth."

They walked the beach leaving long trails of footprints in the silky sand that washed away with the tide. Palm fronds behind the beach left shadows like fingers crawling perpetually across the ground, and as Grey and Misty stepped into the forest to escape the heat of the sun, their own shadows vanished. They watched the bay from the jungle shade, quiet storms drifting on the horizon and dropping curtains of rain on the islands and the sea beyond. Fog crept into the hills from the beach like a creature of its own mind.

From one place on one beach in one day they could observe the full range of the color spectrum. Soft yellow sunrises emerged over the hills and turned to the brightest of blue skies, and the water was crystal clear and gentle, reflecting the mountainous isles and the painted heavens like their world turned upside down. A rich geography of cotton clouds drifted overhead and rained down upon them each day and transformed in the evenings to accentuate passionate pink and purple sunsets that sank into the blackest of nights when the only lights were the countless stars creeping ever so slowly across the sky. Grey and Misty lay on a blanket in the sand, mapping the constellations until they fell asleep, and they dreamed of the very beach where they slept and arose again with the sun and the tide. Pure verdant hills recalled an ancient world of native people with the same needs and the same love but far simpler desires and aspirations. What was left of that world was confined to the most isolated places on the globe—places that people from cities referred to as paradise. But paradise, Misty thought, was more than a physical place. It was also a state of mind—an inner peace just barely within the fathoms of hope for people of such complex circumstances. She kept her faith though. Aside from Grey, faith was all she had left.

# 25

## PATRIOT

"The Coast Guard should have found them by now," said Richter, looking out the window of the West Roosevelt office toward the Chicago skyline and the great blue lake beyond. "I still don't understand how they just vanished on a sailboat."

"They're searching every harbor in the USVI," said McGuinness, "and we're tracking the credit cards they used. Let's focus on what we're doing here. What did you get out of Mancini's nephew?"

"Not much. It took weeks to get him to poke his head out of whatever hole he was hiding in, and he came with his lawyer. He seems to operate a little differently than his late uncle."

"Yeah, the old man wouldn't have brought his lawyer to a first interview. He would have thought it made him look weak."

"Well, the nephew insists that the family is in mourning and not interested in any more death. You know. Says that Sal was legitimate once he got out—told me all about the development project in St. Louis, but he claims he'd never heard the names Grey Cavanaugh or Misty Sommer until they hit news."

"Sounds about right. We don't have anything on him, and the only person even suggesting he was involved is Zanetti."

"Yeah. He did say one thing that I found interesting though," said Richter.

"What's that?"

"He said he heard Francesco De Luca was back in town."

McGuinness froze for a moment and then laughed, hoping that Richter had not noticed his surprise. "That would be interesting," he said.

"Isn't he supposed to be dead?"

"You know," said McGuinness, "sometimes I wonder if these guys aren't all immortal. If you came in here tomorrow and told me that Sal Mancini was in the lobby asking for me, I wouldn't be entirely surprised."

"Well, we should look into it."

"Sure, we'll look into it."

Agent Sanborn walked into the room with three cups of coffee and set them on the desk. McGuinness grabbed one and took a long drink. Steam poured from beneath his nostrils.

"What's up, guys?" she asked, sensing his tension.

"We have a lead," said Richter.

"I wouldn't go so far as to call it a lead," McGuinness interjected. "More of a ghost."

"It's funny you use that term."

"Why?"

"Because that's what the analyst called our sixth shooter."

"You guys want to tell me what you're talking about?" Sanborn asked, taking a sip of her coffee.

"De Luca," said Richter, and she coughed on her drink. "He's back."

Sanborn looked at McGuinness who shrugged and set his cup back on the desk.

"Look," he said, "if it makes you feel better we'll check it out. Let's take a ride over to The Drake this morning."

"The Drake?" asked Richter.

"That's where De Luca used to stay in the good ol' days, but don't get your hopes up. All of our intel suggests that Sal Mancini had him knocked off back in ninety-one before the trial."

The three agents drove to The Drake Hotel and pulled up to the curb behind a line of limousines in front of the elegant awning over the front doors. McGuinness eyed the sculpted golden dragons protruding from the limestone walls and balancing glowing azure orbs upon their heads on either side of the entrance. He had never been one to embrace such gothic adornment. It gave him chills. He considered himself old-fashioned in few ways, progressive in most, and he much preferred contemporary architecture—not the cold, white, angular sort, but the warm and minimalistic style drawn from its natural element. Still he loved The Drake for its memories of days past—days when his work still gave him a thrill and still felt noble and honest. The longer he was on the job the more he knew, and the more he knew the more secrets he kept within.

They left the keys to the Suburban with the valet at the door and walked into the building. Images of golden dragons were mirrored in the carpet on the floor, furious mouths open and wrapped around the shield where the prominent Old English *D* commanded a certain respect of all who entered. To McGuinness, that letter represented a different name—one belonging to the single most dangerous man he had ever known, even more so now that his son was in such peril. A man with dueling identities, the first well known in certain circles of both law enforcement and the criminal underworld, and a second, even more fearsome, known to very few. That man, McGuinness knew, was not to be crossed.

He looked around at the employees and guests as they walked by, none of who had ever heard even a whisper of the secret history of The Drake. Although Declan had, when he lived as Francesco De Luca, once resided in the haunting hotel, McGuinness had no expectation that they would find him there. He had brought Agents Richter and Sanborn simply as a matter of course before moving on to new theories, but as they rose the royal blue staircase to the main lobby his skin turned cold and his heart began to race. There, sitting quietly alone in a corner chair, Declan sat reading. He looked up from his book and directly at Agent McGuinness, and he smiled. McGuinness froze.

"Oh my God."

"What?" asked Sanborn.

"That's him."

Richter put his hand on his gun and reached for his handcuffs with the other.

"Stop," said McGuinness. "He's expecting us. Wait here."

Agent McGuinness approached slowly as Richter and Sanborn stood watch from the top of the staircase. He sat down in the chair opposite a small coffee table from Declan and stared at him for a moment, seeking the first words he would say to the smiling man he had not seen in over twenty-five years. A dead man. A ghost.

"Hello, Francesco."

"Hello, Aldo."

"You know," said McGuinness, "I hadn't heard that name in, well, since the last time I saw you, and this is the second time I've been called that this month. What's that you're reading?"

Declan handed him the book.

"*The Bourne Identity*? Seriously?"

Declan laughed. "Have you read it?"

"No."

"You should," he said, nodding toward the book. McGuinness opened the front cover to find a note inside.

*Take me in.*

He discreetly took the note and slipped it into his jacket pocket and looked up at Declan.

"You'll go quietly?"

Declan smiled again.

"Alright," said McGuinness standing up and turning toward the staircase and Agents Sanborn and Richter. "Let's go."

"No handcuffs?"

"Would they do any good?"

"Probably not."

Declan rose and followed McGuinness, crossing the lobby and walking down the stairs toward the front door with Sanborn and Richter close behind. The four stood on the sidewalk wordlessly waiting for the valet to return with the SUV. When it pulled up to the curb, Declan and McGuinness climbed into the rear seat. McGuinness's leg bounced restlessly as they rode back toward the FBI field office, but Declan was still as a corpse, looking straight ahead at the back of Richter's skull.

The guard at the field office entrance waved them through and the gate closed behind them. Sanborn drove slowly through the campus and down the ramp to the lower level sally port where she swiped her badge and the garage door opened. They pulled through and sat waiting for the door to roll down and seal shut before stepping out. McGuinness winced at the fluorescent lighting high above them.

"Alright, De Luca," said Richter, "arms out."

Declan complied as the young agent took his jacket and patted him down. McGuinness and Sanborn watched their colleague in his naïve confidence, both knowing how quickly their detainee could turn the tables and take all three of their lives. It didn't matter if he was armed. He was no less dangerous without a weapon.

"We're good," said Richter, slapping Declan on the back. "Let's get a room."

Sanborn swiped her badge and the door from the sally port buzzed loudly as it opened to a long hallway. They led Declan to a stark white room with a metal table and two chairs and a one-way mirrored wall.

"Make yourself at home," said Agent Sanborn, closing the door behind her. McGuinness and Richter stepped into the next room to watch. They flipped on the microphone and listened.

"So, Francesco De Luca," came Sanborn's voice through the speaker as Declan took a seat at the table and unbuttoned his shirt cuffs and rolled them up. "We thought you were dead."

"Not yet."

"I've heard about you for a long time, Francesco. It's nice to put a face to the name."

"Likewise."

"Oh yeah?" she asked. "You've heard of me?"

"Sure, Special Agent Sanborn. Your friend McGuinness and I have run into each other once or twice. He mentioned you."

She looked at the glass wall as if she could see McGuinness on the other side, then turned back to Declan.

"What are you doing back in town?"

"Vacationing. Chicago is beautiful this time of year, don't you think?"

"First time back since ninety-one?"

"I don't recall the last time I was here."

"But you were here in ninety-one," she pressed, sitting down at the table across from him.

"If you say so."

"How long have you been in town?"

"A few months I guess. I'm not sure exactly. You'd have to ask the hotel."

"Months? That's quite a vacation."

"I like to watch the seasons change," he said.

"Did you bring any weapons with you?"

"I'm retired," Declan laughed. "I don't much like guns anyway."

"No? I hear you're an impressive marksman."

"Perhaps. But I prefer not to carry weapons. They do more harm than good. Do you agree?"

"My job requires me to carry a weapon."

"But that's not why you do it," said Declan. "You love the hunt. I can see it in your eyes. Conrad is the same way. Perhaps that's why you two get along so well."

She leaned back in her chair.

"What do you mean by that?" she asked.

"That's just what he told me," he replied. He smiled and looked at the mirrored wall.

McGuinness hastily entered the room a few seconds later, followed by Richter who closed the door behind him. Sanborn took the hint and stood from the chair and watched from the corner of the room as McGuinness took the seat across from Declan. The two looked at each other for minutes, the agent with his inquisitive, unflinching stare, and the subject with his sly grin. Each, it seemed, was waiting for the other to speak.

"Francesco," said McGuinness finally, taking a pen from his pocket and clicking it open and shut. He set it on the table with a pad of paper and slid it across to Declan. "I need you to write down the address where you've been living the last twenty-five years."

Declan picked up the pen and clicked it a few times and flipped through the blank sheets.

"I'll need more paper," he laughed.

"Let's start with your current address."

"One Forty East Walton Place, Chicago."

McGuinness shook his head.

"Permanent address," he said impatiently.

"That's as close to permanent as it gets."

"You know why you're here, Francesco," said McGuinness, taking back the pen and clicking it a few more times. "Mafia henchmen are getting picked off in the streets, and then we find out you're back in town. If you want to get out of here then you're going to have to work with us."

Richter shifted nervously in the corner of the room. Sanborn glanced at him, then back at Declan as he shrugged and leaned forward and rested his elbows on the table. She watched him closely, his arms folded in such a way that only she and McGuinness could see his hands. He tapped an index finger discreetly. She watched his pattern.

... --- -- - - .-. .-- ... - .... .. --

*Don't trust him*

Her stance stiffened, but only Declan noticed. He looked at her for a moment, then leaned back in his chair.

"Are you killing for the mob again?" demanded McGuinness, clicking the pen.

.-- .... ---

*Who*

Declan wiped his eyes and clasped his hands behind his head.

"I'm retired," he said, blinking.

*Richter*

Sanborn looked at Richter in her periphery, completely unaware of the parallel conversation.

Declan rubbed his eyes again. "I'm sorry," he said, blinking erratically, "you really should humidify these rooms."

*Lock me up—he'll come to me*

"Cut the shit," said Richter. "We know you're working for the Mancinis again. When the forensics report comes back, we'll have all the proof we need, and then you'll have a target on your head. It doesn't matter to us whether you're dead or in prison, but it's easier for everyone if you talk now. We'll let you think on it. Agent McGuinness, may I speak with you?"

McGuinness stood, and the three agents moved to the next room closing Declan in alone.

"He knows we don't have anything on him," said Sanborn, looking through the glass at the calm assassin on the other side.

"Doesn't matter," replied Richter. "We've got him. Now we build our case. And you thought we'd never find him. The infamous Francesco De Luca is getting sloppy."

"Don't be arrogant," said McGuinness. "We found him because he meant us to."

"Why would he do that?"

"Maybe he's the one who needs protection," Sanborn suggested. "He's safer in here than out there."

"Well," said McGuinness, "if he's our sniper we don't want to put him back on the streets."

"We don't have to," said Richter. "You didn't have the PATRIOT Act in nineteen ninety-one. It doesn't matter if we can charge him or not, he looks good for the sniper attacks. That makes him a suspected terrorist."

"Terrorism?" said Sanborn. "For shooting mobsters? That's a bit of a stretch."

"It doesn't have to stick. It just gives us time to figure out what the hell is going on."

"Alright," said McGuinness, "you said it. Let's lock him up."

He and Sanborn allowed Richter the pleasure of booking Declan at the request of the young agent. Neither of them wished for the bragging rights of arresting the infamous mafia hit man, because they alone knew the truth, and the truth would come out. They left the field office together that evening, headed toward Carla Sanborn's Lakeview greystone. McGuinness had checked out of his hotel room weeks earlier. He set his briefcase on the bench seat in the kitchen and poured two drinks, and they sat at the island and sipped their bourbon by candlelight, looking at one another. Dim light was better for conversation.

"I saw that today," said Carla. "You and De Luca."

"Leave it to a couple of old-timers to communicate in Morse code," Conrad sighed. "So now we know."

"Are you sure we can trust him?"

"Yes."

"You think De Luca—Declan—plans to kill Richter?"

"If I did I wouldn't have left them alone together. I just hope we can cover his ass when this is all over. No matter what happens, he still killed a lot of people."

"Bad people. And besides Declan, only three people know that, and you and I aren't talking."

"Well, now we have an ally," said Conrad, taking a sip of his bourbon. "Now we can get to work."

Declan stood and watched as Richter filled out the intake paperwork in front of him. He did not speak a word as the young agent took his watch and shoes and belt and clasped the handcuffs on his wrists and led him to a windowless basement cell with only a cot and a toilet where he would remain, patiently waiting, until the traitor returned for him. Then he would have his vengeance.

# 26

## United and Isolated

"I still can't reach him," said Grey, holding the sat-phone to his ear.

"You've been trying for days," replied Misty.

"I shouldn't have waited so long."

"Do you think they got to him?"

"I don't know," he said, setting the phone down. He walked to the wall of windows that lined the back of the house in the hills and looked out to the water far below. Misty stood behind him and put her hand on his back.

"You haven't been sleeping well the last few weeks," she said.

"No."

"Tell me what you're thinking."

"Have you been watching the harbor lately?"

"Not closely, no."

"I have," he said. "And I'm seeing a lot of the Coast Guard. I think they're looking for us."

"If Sophie was going to sell us out she would have done it already."

"I have a bad feeling. We're too close. We need to get far away."

"What are you thinking?"

"I don't know. Maybe we should go back and look for him."

"Grey," she said, pressing herself against his back and wrapping her arms around him, "you know we can't do that. We'll never get back into the country."

"What do you suggest?"

"How about the west coast? We can sail to the Panama Canal."

"No," he said, shaking his head. "Too dangerous. Too much procedure and visibility. They'll board the vessel."

"South then. Aruba?"

"What about Cuba or Venezuela? They don't like to extradite."

"That's dangerous, Grey. I'm less concerned about extradition now that we know what kind of reach these mob guys have. If we end up needing the FBI they'll never be able to get to us in those places."

He turned away from the window and looked at her.

"Aruba," he said. "Four hundred fifty nautical miles across the Caribbean Sea."

"So?"

"Alright, I like it."

"How quickly can we get there?"

"Maybe a week."

"I'll call Sophie to get the yacht ready."

Grey watched the harbor from the road as they drove to Sophie's dockyard that evening. Tiny lights dotted the hills, reflected in the black waves of the sea. The Coast Guard had left earlier in the day and boat traffic was light. Only a few fishing vessels still moved on the water. Grey and Misty boarded the *Mistical Reflection* with only the clothes they wore and whatever had been left upon her when they had arrived, and they sailed slowly and quietly out of the harbor as they had from Annapolis on that early morning more than nine months before.

They watched St. Thomas pass in the night and St. Croix in the morning, and soon the turquoise shallows turned to deep navy as they left civilization behind, headed southwest on the surface of the abyss. The clouds that passed over the archipelago disappeared and the sky cleared leaving only a faint haze hovering on the horizon. Without a point of reference it could have been any sea, any ocean on earth. There were no trees or mountains or deserts to hint at their place upon the globe—only the warmth of the Caribbean summer and the smell of saltwater and the deep blue forever.

They furled the jib and raised the spinnaker to catch the east wind and let it push them easily southwest on a consistent broad reach. Misty lay on the deck at the bow and looked up at the massive sail, its transparent indigo sprawling across the sky. She looked through it at the white-hot orb beyond and spread her arms to let her skin absorb the radiance. She closed her eyes and listened to the wooden hull cutting through the sea. Her breath synchronized with the rhythmic waves slipping by on either side of her as the yacht glided gently over them and the mist cooled her.

Again they were alone, both free and trapped, united and isolated. Grey was quiet and distant, always at the helm and focused on the open water ahead as if there were a single obstacle within a hundred miles. The sun would rise and set, but he slept and ate little. It wasn't, Misty suspected, that he wished to reach their destination in a hurry. She understood that it was sailing that brought him the most peace—moving across the sea upon the vessel that he had created from his own vision. He was always on the move, emotionally even when not geographically, and she wished that he could find that same peace in a single place with her as he once had. It seemed asinine to be jealous of an inanimate object, particularly one designed as a reflection of herself. Elegant craft had always been feminine, serving as surrogates for sailors of centuries past who spent months—even years away from the women in their lives. With a woman so close, she thought, Grey should never have been wanting. It felt to her almost as if she were the stand-in when he was not aboard his vessel.

He was awake at the helm each night when she went to sleep, and he was there still when she awoke. On the third morning she rose from the cabin to find him with his arms draped limply through the old ship's wheel and his head pressed against it.

"Grey," she said, grabbing his shoulder, "are you alright?"

He shook his head and opened his eyes.

"What?"

"You need sleep."

"No," he said, standing up and looking toward the bow. "We have to keep moving. They're close behind."

"There's nobody following us. Go to bed. If you really want to keep sailing then I'll take the helm."

"No."

"You're losing it."

"Wouldn't you be?" he asked, turning toward her. "My dad is probably dead, and it's my fault."

"No it's not. Why would you say that?"

"Because it's the truth."

"Did you kill Mancini?" she asked rhetorically.

"I don't know!" he snapped, and she stepped back from him. "Maybe I did. I don't know."

"What do you mean you don't know?"

"You want to know why I can't sleep? I have nightmares—visions of myself stabbing that son of a bitch to death over and over again. That's the closest thing I have to a memory of that night. So yes, I might have done it. I might have killed him."

Misty sat down and looked up at him. She opened her mouth, but she could not conjure words. She could not discern the expression on his face as he looked down upon her, and suddenly she was terrified of him. She looked around at the open sea, then back at Grey.

"Do you still feel safe with me?" he asked.

"Of course," she replied, the tone of her voice less confident than her words.

"You know I would never hurt you."

"Yes."

He turned back to the helm. Misty went to the bow and sat watching the horizon rise and fall for hours. The wind picked up throughout the day, and the sea grew rough. By nightfall they were riding fifteen-foot swells. Grey remained at the helm with the spinnaker full as Misty tossed in the cabin below, drifting in and out of sleep. She awoke in the morning to the sound of Grey howling from above, and she stumbled up the stairs as the yacht rocked wildly.

"Grey!" she yelled over the sound of the wind.

"What?"

"What are you yelling about?"

"The trade winds!" he shouted back. "They're awesome!"

She climbed to the deck and held tight to the rails as the *Mistical Reflection* crashed through the waves. When she reached the bench at the helm she fell onto it and gripped the gunwale to keep from going overboard. Ahead she saw the rocky cliffs of Aruba's north shore and the white mist of breakers colliding violently.

"We can't anchor here," she said as a wave rolled beneath them and the yacht keeled suddenly to the port side where she sat, lifting her off the bench. She screamed and Grey dove and grabbed her with his left hand to keep her from dumping over the side, still holding onto the wheel with his right. He laughed like a hyena and goose bumps ran down her arms.

"Having fun yet?" he asked.

"No," she said. "This is too much. Take down the spinnaker. We're almost there."

"Not yet."

"You want to crash into the cliffs?"

He laughed at the sky and she scrambled to open the compartment beneath her seat for a life vest. She struggled to put it on, holding fast to the boat as it rocked in the ferocious sea. The sun was bright and hot and there was not a single cloud above them, but the intensity of the trade winds made for a wild sail.

Grey veered the vessel from a southwest heading to due west running before the wind with the spinnaker full and picking up speed. Misty moved to the starboard bench and watched the barren desert landscape moving alongside. There was not a person in sight—only black boulders and dry red earth under a haze of dust. As they drew near the shore they passed the California Lighthouse on the north point of the island and came about and rounded the point and took a southern heading and the sea suddenly calmed.

"Now we can drop the spinnaker," said Grey. He released the sheets as Misty pulled and packed the indigo sail and then unfurled the jib. Her racing heart slowed and she took off the life vest as they cruised along the southwest side of the island and civilization emerged. Resorts dotted the coastline and people filled the white beaches beneath thatched umbrellas and canopies.

"Where do we anchor?" asked Misty.

"There's a lagoon south of Oranjestad. I called Ankur. Everything is settled with the Aruba Ports Authority."

"I hope none of this comes back on him," she sighed.

"We need to worry about ourselves," he replied. "We're the ones in real danger."

# 27

# Always a Way Out

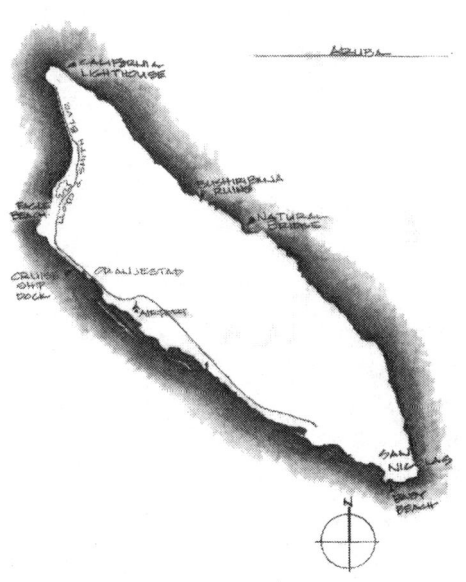

The days were hot and bright and long under the intense South Caribbean sun. Rain rarely came, and when it did it lasted only a few moments and the sun never left, but the wind was unremitting. Grey and Misty lived in anonymity, hiding in plain sight amongst the population. They spent nights on the yacht and rose each morning and paddled to shore where they wandered the streets of Oranjestad with its brightly colored Dutch Caribbean architecture and palm trees. They walked north toward the beaches and miles of resorts lining the south shore of the island where the water was cerulean and calm, and they ran each day in the sand and the wind. Wild dogs slept in burrows in the shade of Divi Divi trees that grew out of the white beaches, their gnarled gray trunks leaning southwest and thick green canopies sprawling as if reaching for a taste of the sea.

Misty found solace in her daily runs as Grey did on his yacht. When she ran she was in control, focused and determined, and she would not stop running until her mind was clear and her fear had been subdued. The breeze cooled the sweat on her skin as her shadow glided across the sand ahead of Grey's, but he stayed with her, never letting her out of his sight. He would never let her go, she knew. At one time that knowledge had brought her comfort, but now it made her uneasy. She had become less certain of his intentions. But she knew him well. He was not a violent man, and she knew that he would never kill unless his own life, or hers, was in danger. Even if he had killed Mancini to protect her, she wondered why he would not say it, and he seemed to draw away from her and from reality now whenever he raised the sails of the *Mistical Reflection*. On the land, though, she saw in him more of the man she had known before, and so she was content to stay while they could.

For weeks they moved from one expensive meal to the next, paying in cash and rarely considering its draining supply or what they would do when it was gone. They ate seafood on beaches by torchlight with their bare feet in the sand, and they walked miles on the dark road back to the lagoon where they would paddle back out to the yacht and Grey would try Declan again and again and then drink until he fell asleep. Misty watched him fighting his fear but never speaking of it. Whispers of a tropical storm to the north left her feeling even more trapped, and she wondered how long they could keep their secret living so visibly on this tiny island.

Cruise ships docked at the marina as they watched from the second floor veranda of a bar across the street. It was a sunny afternoon, as every afternoon had been, and Misty saw on Grey's face a rare calm and a smile that reminded her how much she loved him. He looked down at the road below and the line of shop huts between the traffic and the water where local artisans filled tables and walls with their crafts and trinkets. Colorful flags billowed in the wind alongside the road. He took a sip of his drink and looked back at her, and they gazed at each other.

"You seem better today," she said.
"Yeah?"
"Yeah."
"I think it's the running," he laughed.

"I told you it's addictive. It's a good addiction. Cleanses the body. I'll make you a marathoner yet."

"You're always trying to fix me."

"Only the things that need fixing," she said.

"What happens when you've fixed everything? Will I be perfect then?"

"You're perfect now."

His eyes saddened and he looked away. "I'm trying," he said.

She scooted her chair closer to him and reached out and touched his cheek, and he looked back up at her.

"I miss you," she said.

"Me too."

Behind Misty, three members of a cruise ship crew dressed in white uniforms came through the open doors of the bar and sat down at the table next to them. Grey eyed the insignia on their shoulders—two cadets and a third officer. They ordered drinks and appetizers and Grey and Misty listened as they quipped about the weather to the north.

"Maybe a few days at port will give my stomach a chance to settle," said a young cadet.

"You'll get used to it," said the third officer. "That was just a little chop."

Misty turned toward them.

"Did you guys just get in this morning?"

"We did," said the third officer. "This lubber here is still working on his sea legs."

"Where did you come from?" she asked.

"St. Kitts. We hit some weather from the tropical storm on our way out. It made a bit of a mess on the ship. You two are from the States, right?"

"Yes," said Grey.

"You fly here?"

"We sailed."

Misty touched his knee beneath the table to stop him from saying anything further.

"A man after my own heart," said the third officer. "Well, I hope you're not planning on heading home any time soon. It'll be a hurricane by the time it reaches the Gulf."

"No," said Misty, looking at Grey. "We'll be around awhile."

They finished their drinks and walked down the wide curving staircase to the street. They walked the trail along the edge of the marina past the luxury shops and the marketplace and restaurants they had already visited and detoured through Wilhelmina Park, following paths beneath towering palms, and they stood gazing at the blue horizon beyond the boulders and sunbathing iguanas. Then they crossed the bridge over the canal and walked along the beach until they reached the Aruba Surfside Marina and went through the gate, across the brick patio, and followed the boardwalk out over the water to Pinchos at the end of the pier.

They got a table and drank some more while they watched the blue sky fade to orange and then black as the sun set leaving the flickering glow of candles and the blue lights of the bar pavilion and the stars above them. Misty watched shadows dancing across Grey's face from the lantern between them. In the night the wind softened to a breeze and the air cooled, and she put her hands behind her head and lifted her hair from her neck to dry the sweat.

"Sounds like it's a good thing we left the Virgin Islands when we did," she said.

"Yeah."

"We would have been trapped there with the storm."

"There's always a way out," he replied. "Sometimes it's just harder to find."

"Is that what you've been thinking about?"

"What?"

"A way out."

"Aren't you?"

"It's getting late," she said. "We should get dinner."

The server came and they ordered and the spread was elegant and delicious as every meal had been. It seemed there was not a bad restaurant on the island, but perhaps they had only been to the best. Grilled shrimp and salmon and mahi-mahi and grouper had become staples of their diet. By the time they were finished the wait staff was clearing the last table and closing down the bar. Grey took out his wallet and opened it to pay the bill. He looked inside and laughed.

"We don't have enough cash," he said.

"You think they have an ATM?"

"No. We'll get more tomorrow if we can still access the accounts. I'm hoping they're still good after what happened in St. Thomas."

"Then how do we pay for dinner?"

"Credit card."

"I guess we're done living off the grid," she said.

"It was only a matter of time."

"And what if we can't access the bank accounts?"

"I guess we'll see."

They paid the bill and walked quietly back to the tranquil lagoon. Grey remained awake on the yacht's deck throughout the night, watching the faint black horizon, and he was still there when the sun broke over the island and Misty rose from the cabin below. She dove over the side into the water barely leaving a ripple as she disappeared beneath the surface and then reemerged. Grey watched her from his seat at the helm. Her skin glistened in the morning light as she swam laps around the hull to wake herself up. She paddled back to the ladder and climbed aboard again panting and dripping onto the deck, and she walked to the bow and sprawled out on her back to dry in the sun.

Grey stood and followed her to the bow. He lay down beside her, propped on his elbow, and looked down at her.

"You're blocking my sun," she said, smiling.

He ran his fingertips through her hair and down her cheek, and he leaned in and kissed her.

"Let me know when you're ready to go into town," he said. He wrapped his arms around her and rested his head. Soon he fell into a deep sleep, and Misty could not bear to disturb him. She left him lying in the sun on the deck and wrote a note for him to find when he awoke, but it had been so long since he had been able to sleep in peace that she suspected he would still be there when she returned. She paddled to shore alone and withdrew cash from an ATM and took a cab to Eagle Beach where she went for a short run, seeking the comfort of solitude. But comfort did not come. Even now, without Grey she felt empty. The more desperate he seemed the less she trusted him to be alone, and she nearly forgot that he had all but confessed to murder. Her love for him was stronger than her fear. She stopped for groceries at the market on her way back to the lagoon, and when she climbed back onto the deck Grey had not moved in the hours of her absence.

More days passed and nothing changed. It must have been a Monday as the weekend crowds had died down in the downtown malls and markets. They hailed a cab to take them to the Palm Beach district and climbed inside. The car rolled slowly through Oranjestad, but when the traffic cleared on Lloyd G. Smith Boulevard the driver hit the accelerator hard, whipping between lanes and around other cars on the road.

"Slow down!" Grey yelled.

"You're being followed," said the driver. They turned and looked out the rear window to see two Jeeps in the distance gaining on them. Tires squealed as the car swerved through traffic and palm trees and *Aloe* plants passed by in a blur. Grey looked back ahead and the driver took off his hat.

"Tobias? How did you—"

"Do you still have the gun I gave you?"

Misty reached in her purse and pulled out the 1911.

"Good," he said. "Is it loaded?"

"Full magazine," said Grey.

"There's a Glock under the seat in front of you. Take it."

Grey reached beneath the seat and pulled out the pistol. The engine roared as they sped into the Palm Beach district and Tobias swerved to avoid pedestrians crossing the street. The Jeeps in pursuit were less careful and continued to draw near. Past the last high-rise the road opened up again and the car raced at top speed up the desert road along the edge of the calm blue sea.

"Do you have a boat?" asked Misty.

"I didn't have time," said Tobias. "We'll have to outrun them. Or kill them."

Up ahead they saw the California Lighthouse. The car circled past the north side of it and whipped around the last corner at the end of the road and skidded to a stop in front of the tower. A tour group stopped taking pictures and turned their attention to the stolen cab. Tobias got out, leaving the engine running, and Grey and Misty followed.

"We'll never lose them on the road. We need another vehicle." He looked around, then pointed to an extended

Land Rover Defender retrofitted for group safari tours. "That one."

The two Jeeps came tearing into the dusty lot as Grey and Misty ran toward the Land Rover. Tobias ducked behind the stolen cab and drew his gun. "Keep running!" he yelled as he began firing. The mobsters in the Jeeps fired back and sightseers dropped to the ground screaming. A man with a machete hid behind a wooden booth where he had been chopping the tops off coconuts for tourists to drink their water. Grey snatched the blade from his hand as they ran by. They dove into the Land Rover and ducked for cover as bullets whizzed past, and Grey's instincts from those years of training with his father began to take over. The scene appeared in slow motion, and he drafted a blueprint in his head—not of a building, but of a course of action.

"What about Tobias?" asked Misty.

"I'm going back for him," said Grey, shifting into first and hitting the gas. The rear end whipped around and they barreled back into the line of fire. Misty held the 1911 out the window and squeezed the trigger. Sparks flew as metal struck metal and windows shattered. Zanetti's men took cover behind their vehicles.

"Get in!" Misty yelled as they scraped to a stop in the dirt beside Tobias. He darted from behind the car and ran toward them, and then a shot came echoing off the lighthouse. Tobias stumbled. He took three more labored steps, and he fell face down in the dust. "No!" she screamed. She opened the door to reach him, but before she could step out Grey hit the accelerator again.

"What are you doing? He could still be alive!"

"He's gone, Misty. Hold on and get your head down."

They both ducked behind the dashboard to dodge the rain of bullets coming at them as Grey drove directly toward the shooters. He rammed the front Jeep and Zanetti's thugs scattered as it rolled over onto its side, and he sped off the road and onto an unpaved path toward the northeast side of the island. Misty looked through the cloud of dust behind them where Tobias lay motionless in the dirt.

The second Jeep quickly gave chase, following them down the north shoreline where the sound of the deep blue waves crashing into the cliffs was drowned out by the wind and the roaring V8 engine. The tires ground around sharp twists and turns at the base of the red mountainside, but Grey was ruthless behind the wheel. He would not slow.

"If they get close, you shoot them," he said.

She looked at him, and he looked back. The expression on his face was one of blazing fury. It was the expression of a killer.

"Not just *at* them, Misty. You aim for the chest. You hear me?"

She nodded.

"Tell me you hear me."

"I hear you," she said, the gun in her hand shaking with her fear.

She watched the Jeep through the dust in the rear view, shredding the path in pursuit.

"Do you know where you're going?" she asked.

"Yes."

"Where?"

"Trust me."

"You're making that very difficult. You're scaring me."

"You should be scared," he said. "Hold on."

He turned sharply and dropped into second, bounding up the mountainside and leaving the coast behind them. The tires slipped and rolled across boulders, but the Rover was as relentless as its driver, bowling upward on three wheels and angles that Grey hoped would dump the stock Jeep behind them. Still it followed.

Misty peered between the seats and pointed the pistol beneath the rippling canopy over the passenger compartment behind them. She aimed for the driver, but the ride was far too rough for any accuracy. She fired anyway, and they fired back. Shot after deafening shot popped in both directions, and she did not stop until she had emptied the magazine.

"I can't hit anything like this," she said.

Grey turned the wheel and pounded the gas pedal, whipping the Rover around in the opposite direction. "Get your head down!" he yelled as he pulled out the Glock. They barreled back down the mountain directly at the pursuing Jeep. Bullets shattered the windshield and ripped off the side view mirror. Smoke poured from beneath the hood.

"Grey!" Misty screamed. "Are you crazy?"

He turned again sharply just before they collided, and as they came alongside Zanetti's men Grey hit the brakes and lifted the gun and pointed it directly into their wide-open cab. Misty ducked her head between her knees and covered it with her hands. The adrenaline pumping through her veins had sent every sense into a hyperactive state. Flashes came like fireworks behind her eyelids. She could smell the burning gunpowder, leaking gasoline, and the smoke pouring from the pierced engine block. She could hear each bullet as it hissed through the air and each strike on the metal vehicle panels and the screams of grown men in agony. She felt the heat of every explosion and tasted the dust floating in the dry air. She opened her eyes just slightly, but enough to see the blood spatter in the Jeep through the black smoke, and suddenly the Rover lunged forward, shredding the landscape on its way back down the mountainside.

"Are you OK?" Grey asked.

She could not speak.

"Misty!"

"Yes," she stammered. She looked behind them and saw two bodies being pushed out of the Jeep before it turned to follow once more.

"You killed them."

"Good," he said. "How many left."

"Looks like one—no, two."

He threw the Glock out the window.

"We're out of rounds."

They hit the path again and sped on along the coast. They passed the Bushiribana ruins with their strange stacks of rocks laid out like a crop field that disappeared quickly behind them. The path weaved through the rugged desert landscape, but the blue horizon to the northeast did not change. Soon the Jeep was again drawing near.

"Where are you going," asked Misty.

"The bridge."

"The bridge?"

"The natural bridge."

The engine sputtered and began to slow. Grey pushed the accelerator to the floor, but it was no use. Zanetti's henchmen raced up behind them. More shots whizzed by, and Grey swerved in front of the Jeep to keep it from pulling alongside.

"There it is," he said. "Up ahead."

"What's your plan?"

"Get ready to roll. We're jumping."

"What?"

"Just go when I tell you."

The Jeep rammed them from behind and they lurched forward. Then again.

"Get ready," said Grey as they swerved into the lot aimed directly at the cliff left by the collapsed limestone arch. Misty reached for her door handle and Grey for his, and he grabbed the machete with his other hand. "Now!" he yelled as the Jeep rammed them one final time and they plowed through the safety barricade. They threw open their doors and bailed from either side of the Rover, tucking and rolling on the rough ground, and a second later both vehicles disappeared over the edge.

Without hesitation or emotion Grey stood and stumbled toward Misty and lifted her from the ground. He pulled her toward a cluster of parked ATVs and raised the machete into the air as a sign to clear the way. Surrounding sightseers silently obliged.

"Get on," he said, swinging a leg over the seat.

Misty climbed on behind him and wrapped her arms around him. She felt a warm and thick moisture on his abdomen, and she pulled her hand away and looked at her palm. It was covered in blood.

"Grey," she said, "you're shot!"

"Yes."

"We have to get you to a hospital."

"No," he said, starting the motor. "I'm fine."

"You're not fine. You're bleeding all over the place."

"I'm fine."

He sped off into the hillside through the cacti and *Aloe vera* and sparse desert vegetation. The sun beat down upon them without the shade of the palms found almost exclusively along the south shore. They poured sweat. Misty tasted the salt and gunpowder on her upper lip. A burro stood by and watched them pass trailing a dusty haze as they rolled down the hills on the west side and back into the outskirts of town.

"Where are we going?" asked Misty as Grey steered the ATV along paved residential roads.

"Out of here. Back to the yacht."

"Where do you plan on sailing?"

"Home," he said. "I'm done waiting. I'm done running."

"Grey, you've been shot."

"I told you I'm fine."

"And the hurricane?"

"It's not a hurricane."

"You heard what that ship crew told us."

"We can keep west," he said, "follow the coast. We'll wrap around the Yucatán and avoid the storm. By the time it passes we can head to Galveston, New Orleans, Tampa, wherever. But we have to get out of here before more of those guys show up."

"That will be weeks!"

"She can take it."

"But you can't. Not with a bullet in you."

"We have no choice."

"You said there's always a way out."

"Yes. And this is it."

Grey stopped the stolen ATV in the sand at the lagoon. He slashed the lashings holding their kayaks to the pier with the machete and they paddled painfully and laboriously out to the *Mistical Reflection* and climbed aboard. He weighed anchor and motored out of the lagoon and raised the sails leaving footprints of his own blood on the deck while Misty paced in the cabin below, and by sunset they could not see even a glow of civilization on the horizon. She had never felt so alone.

# 28

## Captive

The cell lock clapped open, echoing around four empty stone walls. Declan sat on the edge of the cot and watched the door as Richter came through and closed it again behind him.

"It's about time," said Declan.

"Tell me what you know about Grey Cavanaugh."

"Suddenly you're in a hurry, Special Agent Richter? No chit-chat to warm me up?"

"I'm not in a patient mood."

"That's a shame," said Declan, leaning back against the wall. "They say that patience is a virtue, which must make impatience a vice."

"Don't play games with me."

"Forgive me. You've got me locked up without cause. I'm beginning to lose my sense of humor."

"You want to get out of here?" asked Richter.

"What do you think?"

"Then give me answers."

"About Grey Cavanaugh? What makes you think I know anything about him?"

"I know you're involved in this war that's going on, so you must be looking for him too. Don't you want to help us catch the guy who killed your boss?"

Declan laughed. "I wasn't working for Sal Mancini," he said. "And you and I both know that Grey Cavanaugh didn't kill him."

Richter leaned down nose to nose with Declan.

"Then who did?" he asked.

"You did."

Richter stepped back and looked at him.

"You'd better be careful with accusations like that. I'm a federal agent."

"It doesn't matter anyway," said Declan. "I know you turned the camera and mic off in this room before you came in. You don't want anyone knowing you're here talking to me in the middle of the night. So, let me tell you what I do know. Gianni Zanetti hired me because of your ineffectiveness, and the longer you keep me locked up in here the longer your fall guy keeps sailing around the Caribbean. You've already failed. When Zanetti finds out that you're the one who kept me from doing my job, well, I don't need to tell you how bad that will be for you."

Richter began pacing the cell nervously. "You're full of shit," he said.

"Then keep working on your own," Declan shrugged. "See where that gets you. Or you could give him a call. Tell him I say hi. Zanetti lost faith in you months ago. Why do you think he sent guys down to St. Thomas behind you? Moral support? Then you just stumbled over each other and made a scene."

"How am I supposed to get you out of here now? That would raise all sorts of questions."

"That's not my problem."

Richter stopped pacing and pressed his head against the wall. "Cavanaugh used the credit card again," he said. "Same one he used in St. Thomas. He's in Aruba."

"When?"

"A few days ago."

"Then you'd better get me out of here quick."

"I already gave the information to Zanetti. He sent another crew to take care of it, but we know how well that's worked in the past."

Declan sighed.

"I wish you had come to me first."

# 29

## September

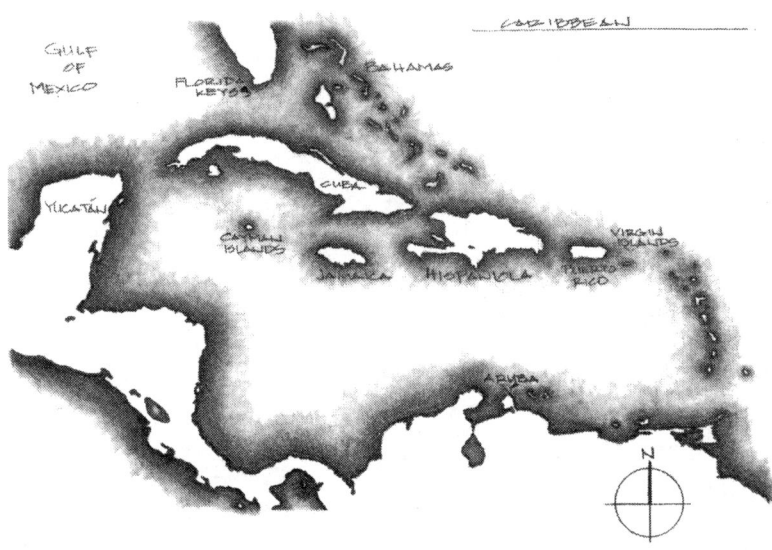

The sky was a grim gray showing less sun each day as they sailed northwest. In four days as they neared Jamaica and the east wind shifted north, Grey lowered the spinnaker and raised the genoa to maintain as much speed as they could now tacking into the wind. Three days later they were passing the Cayman Islands. Misty watched the sky, clouds churning above and a cold light rain falling.

"The winds are calming," she said.

"Yes."

"But the storm looks so close."

"Don't you prefer a smooth sail?" said Grey, resting against the ship's wheel to ease the stress on his wound. The bandages wrapped around his abdomen had gone from white to crimson, and Misty hoped that the bleeding had finally stopped.

"It's eerie," she said. "Makes me nervous."

"Don't be."

"You're looking worse, Grey. We can still get to a hospital. Cancún is a couple days away."

"No. I'll be fine until we're back in the States."

"The storm is a hurricane now," she said, "and it's headed into the Gulf. Unless you want to sail directly into it, we won't be back in the States for weeks. You can't wait that long; there's no exit wound. You need surgery."

"I said no."

Soon he faded from consciousness and Misty took the helm, watching him always to be sure he was still breathing. She took a course toward the Yucatán to be near the shore despite Grey's refusal. If he did not wake up she would have to make decisions for both of them. She feared his reaction when he learned of their proximity to the land, but she feared more that he would sleep into the storm and never wake again.

The sky blackened and the water grew rough as they sailed between Cancún and the west end of Cuba, but still she pushed on. She watched the weather map on the GPS, the hurricane sweeping across southern Florida, and she began to bear west around the peninsula, reaching to seek shelter from the incoming storm on the other side. The blue sky appeared, and she felt a fleeting relief. Grey, though, seemed acutely aware of their position even in his waning capacity, and he rose again to take back his seat.

"I have it," he said as Misty reluctantly moved to the side. "Jibe-ho!"

"Grey, no," she protested, but he ignored her as if he had not heard. He jibed sharply and the genoa whipped to port and filled again quickly, and he swung the stern around pointing the yacht to windward on a close-hauled starboard tack, leaving the blue sky behind and veering directly toward the darkest part of the storm to the east. He cranked in the sheet and the wind turned fierce, whipping across the deck. Misty looked at him, a grin of madness on his face as he drove fast toward the blackened sky. Rain began to pour down upon them.

"That's more like it!" he yelled.

"What happened to keeping west around the Gulf coast?"

"I changed my mind. If we're headed back to the States the Keys are much closer."

"This is insane!"

"She can take it. It's just a little rain."

"Grey," she screamed, pointing into the storm dead ahead, "that's a fucking hurricane!"

"Hold on. It may get rough."

Within hours massive waves were pouring over the gunwales as the hull crashed through them, each one collapsing like a stone wall around a wrecking ball. They heeled violently in the winds but Grey never faltered, even as the bullet inside him tore flesh with his every movement.

"You have to stop this," Misty screamed as she tussled with her life vest and tried to hold on. "At least take down the genoa."

"We're faster with the genoa."

"That's what I'm afraid of. You can't play chicken with a hurricane!"

"We're just skipping along the edge of the storm," he said, "letting the winds carry us. We'll be through this in no time. Don't worry."

"Don't worry?"

"It'll be over soon."

"Yeah, because we'll be dead!"

She looked around at the dark clouds and the wild sea, no longer a hint of blue anywhere, and she realized the depth of their peril. The storm had overtaken them. There was no way out.

"Grey," she pleaded, "I don't want to die out here."

"Then hold on tight!"

The next wave was followed by a trough so deep that the sea seemed to be swallowing them whole. She gripped the rails as tightly as she could, but still her wet hands slipped and she went sliding down the deck toward the bow. Grey dove after her, releasing the wheel, and they began to roll. Suddenly the next wave caught the hull and pulled the bow toward the sky, and Misty came sliding back again. He caught her before she went over the side and held her tight.

"Take this," he said, handing her a line and lashing the other end to the railing. "Tie it to your vest."

"How did I get myself into this?"

"What?"

"Stuck on a boat in a hurricane with a killer who cares nothing for me! Nothing!"

"We're in this together."

"No, Grey. You're in this alone. You just dragged me along."

With those words she saw in his eyes the most pain she had ever seen in the eyes of another person. She saw the moment that he realized what he had done and the sober humanity still buried within him made its way back to the surface. He dropped the sheets and the sails luffed, but they both knew it was too late.

"I trusted you!" she screamed. "I trusted you to take care of me the way I've taken care of you. What a fool I am."

"I can turn us around."

"No you can't, not in these winds! We're dead! Do you understand that? You can add both our lives to your death toll. Maybe they'll name this hurricane after you.

Hurricane Grey! Of course, then someone would have to know where we are. But they don't, do they, Grey?"

"Misty—"

"No, nobody knows where we are! Why? Because we're running from everyone! *Everyone!* Because you're a killer! I'm calling the Coast Guard. We're only a couple hundred miles from Florida. Maybe someone else will care enough to try and save us."

She untied the line from her vest and ran down into the cabin with Grey close behind. Doors and cabinets swung open and shut and dishes were shattered all over the floor, pieces of them sliding around as the yacht pitched about. Water spilled down the steps from the deck above. Misty sat at the VHF radio, switched to channel sixteen, and grabbed for the microphone as she looked at the GPS beside her.

"Mayday! Mayday! Mayday! This is the *Mistical Reflection, Mistical Reflection, Mistical Reflection.* Mayday, this is the *Mistical Reflection.* We are twenty-three degrees eleven thirty-seven north, eighty-five degrees twelve forty west, one hundred seventy-five miles due west of Havana, Cuba. We are trapped in the hurricane and in need of immediate rescue. We are taking on water and will not remain upright. Two adults on board. *Mistical Reflection* is a fifty-foot wooden-hulled sailboat. Over."

She lifted her feet from the water on the floor and waited a moment for a response, then she repeated her call.

"We're way too far out to reach the Coast Guard on the radio," said Grey as he rifled through the open cabinets and the mess on the floor.

"Well we have to do something!" she yelled. "Maybe there's some other crazy asshole out here close enough to hear it."

"You're better off trying the satphone."

She grabbed for the satellite phone. The Coast Guard emergency number had been programmed into the second speed dial, but her shaking finger accidentally hit the first. She listened as it rang and Grey continued rummaging through the mess of their belongings strewn about the cabin.

"What the hell are you looking for?"

"It's here somewhere," he said.

"What's here? Grey, you've lost it. Get your life vest on."

"I have to find it."

"Whatever it is, it doesn't matter. We need to get out of here."

He ran into the berth, splashing through the rising water. He ripped away the sheets and tore through the closet and pulled out every drawer. Misty covered her free ear to block out the sounds of the storm and Grey's commotion, listening only to the seemingly endless ringing through the phone. Then the ringing stopped and she heard a voice on the other end.

"Where are you?"

"Declan?"

"Where are you?" he said again.

She gave their coordinates but heard no response, and she looked at the screen on the phone blinking *low battery*.

"Grey!" she screamed.

"Found it!"

"We have to get out of here now!"

He darted out of the berth and grabbed her arm and pulled her up the steps to the deck. Water flooded across the wood planking as enormous waves crashed over them on all sides. Grey grabbed the mainsheet in a final hopeless attempt to start turning them around, but just as he pulled it taut a squall caught the sail and the yacht heeled. They began to roll and he released the sheet, both of them holding onto the wheel to keep from going over, but the mast could no longer bear the incessant beating. With a deafening crack it snapped, ripped off the yacht and swallowed by the sea. The sheet followed, burning through his palm gripped tightly around it.

Grey crawled to the storage compartment at the helm and threw it open. He pulled out a flare gun and fired it into the air, the brief flash lighting up the churning storm clouds. Then he found another life vest and held on, focused on the compass inlay in the decking, the sea rushing by in his periphery as the needle spun, seeking direction. But there was no course to freedom. For once, there was no way out.

"Misty," he said, "I'm so sorry."

She looked at him with terror in her eyes, terror that he had driven her to, but still she could not bring herself to hate him. Of the countless things he had made her feel—the excitement, the fear, the loneliness, helplessness, joy, fury, and bravery—there was one that trumped all the rest, even as she glared into the eye of her fate.

"I love you," she said as another gale struck and they rolled to the side.

"I love you," he replied.

It had been a journey unlike any they had known before, or ever expected to know. In all this time they had spent with only each other and the endless ocean as company, their love had suffered and fought relentlessly against the odds and their nefarious pursuers, always beating back like the waves against the hull and only a few steps behind at every moment. By the wind and sea their spirits had traveled, and by the same they would depart. As the squall overtook the *Mistical Reflection* and she began to turn over, Grey and Misty spun through the events that had led them to this place, this time, where and when they were both certain they would share their final moments together.

"Grey," she yelled as her grip began to slip, "I can't hold on!"

"Reach for me!"

She held onto the wheel and extended her arm as he reached back, gripping the opposite gunwale with his shredded hand, stretching his torso and tearing open the bullet wound and looking down upon her and the vicious sea below pulling her back. He fought the unconscionable pain and grabbed her fingertips, holding as tight as he could.

"Misty!" he yelled, looking down into her knowing eyes.

"Grey—"

The waves sucked her in, and she disappeared into the mist. Without hesitation he released his grip on the gunwale and dove in after her. He paddled with every bit of strength he had left, screaming her name over and over again, staying afloat by the vest hanging off of his arm. He heard nothing—nothing but the sounds of wind and water and cracking wood. The waves pulled him under, but he fought back, searching the blackness for her.

"Misty!" he yelled, his lungs filling with fluid.

Riding the crest of a swell he saw a glimpse of her pink life vest and went after it. He paddled hard, toppled by the sea, barely able to catch a breath, but he fought on. He fought for her life. Reaching her was the only thing that mattered.

"Grey!" she screamed back, her voice faint and distant.

He watched as she rose, carried toward him by a breaking sea, and he released the vest keeping him at the surface and dove under to fight the current before it reached him and emerged again in the trough.

"I'm coming for you!" he yelled, unable to see her past the next swell, and he dove under again, then again as he drew nearer to the sound of her voice. His eyes burned and he tasted the sea.

"Grey!"

"I'm coming! Hold on!"

He paddled again to the surface and clutched her vest just as she swept by. She pulled him in and wrapped her arms around him and held him close.

"Don't let go," she said.

They turned and looked through the torrential rain and saw the *Mistical Reflection*, toppled and broken, rolling in the fierce sea. Water rushed into the shattered butterfly hatches and filled the cabin. Her bow went under first, gently raising her stern into the air. Tatters of the sails still attached swirled around the hull and faded into obscurity, and Grey watched his precious ship's wheel spinning as waves crashed on the rudder again and again. It was still spinning as it went below, sinking once more to the aquatic underworld from which it had been rescued. Then she disappeared, and the two of them were alone with the sea and the storm.

"Misty," he said, "I don't think I'm going to make it."

"Don't say that, Grey. Stay with me."

"I'm so tired."

"Grey, stay with me."

"I'm sorry for what I said about going down with the ship. I never wanted that."

"It's OK," she said. "It will all be OK."

"I'm too weak. I can't hold on."

"Then I'll hold on to you. I won't let you go. This vest can keep us both afloat."

"I love you."

"I love you."

His eyes closed and his breathing slowed, but Misty held him tight. She whispered into his ear, "You'll be home soon. I love you."

In the distant sky she saw a searchlight, followed by the sound of a helicopter.

# 30

## Reflections

Rising out of the water, holding tight to the cable suspended from above, the whopping of the rotor was deafening like a machine gun. Spotlights flashed across the wild sea below. Voices were muffled by the wind, tossed about in the turbulent air as the winch reeled in the line and the diver pulled through the open door.

The long white hull of the Coast Guard Cutter became visible outside as the rain began to calm, its heavy red and narrow blue stripes near the bow like a flag of salvation breaking through the vicious sea. The Jayhawk rocked about as the pilot arduously set it down on the aft landing deck.

The road was seemingly endless, islands connected by long bridges, water just beyond the palm trees on either side, glimmering and blue under the clearing sky. The truck wound through debris and devastated buildings and work crews, lights flashing and sirens blaring.

Grey opened his eyes and looked around from the hospital bed. His hand and torso were wrapped in bandages, and every muscle movement was strained either from fatigue or the drugs pumping through the IV. Seagulls screeched outside, and he looked out the window at the placid sea.

"Where am I?"

"Key West," said Declan, sitting in the chair beside him.

"Where's Misty? Is she OK?"

"She's fine. She just went to get something to eat."

"She can't be alone. There are people after us."

"Don't worry. She's with Agents McGuinness and Sanborn."

"What?" said Grey, wincing as he sat up.

"Relax. Nobody's coming after you here. She's safe."

"You're sure?"

"Quite."

"Dad, I have to ask you something."

"Yes?"

"Will you take care of her while I'm in prison?"

Declan laughed. "You're not going to prison."

"But I killed Salvatore Mancini."

"Is that what you think?"

"Shouldn't I?"

Misty stepped through the door and her face lit up when she saw that Grey was awake. She ran to him and wrapped her arms around his neck, and he held her close.

"You're really awake this time?" she asked.

"I think so," he said as McGuinness and Sanborn came through the door. "What's going on? Are they here to arrest me?"

Misty looked to Declan.

"Grey," he said, "Agent McGuinness is an old friend of mine. We worked together a long time ago to take down Salvatore Mancini when the Agency learned that he was laundering money for an international terrorist enterprise. I can't give you details, but in order to keep the operation secret the Agency handed Mancini over to the FBI once the laundering operation had been neutralized. At the time, he was only charged with offenses related to organized crime in the States. My cover was blown while I was working with his organization in Libya though, and Mancini learned my real name. He never forgot it. When he got out he wanted to hit me where it hurt."

"So he came after me," said Grey.

"Yes. His ultimate plan was to establish a new smuggling and money laundering operation filtered through the building you designed, the Star Silo, then sell it to his competitor, Gianni Zanetti, and let you go down as a co-conspirator when it was exposed. His people had already been pitching the sale to Zanetti, but he didn't bite. Instead, he saw an opportunity to take out Mancini without leaving his own fingerprints by setting you up for his murder. He found out that Mancini was going to fire you that night, so it was plausible that you would kill him. The only thing Zanetti knew about you was that you made a perfect patsy."

"But I didn't do it?"

"No."

"How do you know?" asked Grey. "Why don't I remember anything from that night in Chicago?"

"You remember Special Agent Richter?"

"Yes."

"He was on Zanetti's payroll. He drugged you in Chicago, murdered Mancini, and planted all the evidence pointing to you. He was supposed to arrest you shortly thereafter. Then you were to be killed in a prison brawl and nobody would ask any more questions."

"My God."

"When you disappeared, that plan became much more difficult. That's when Zanetti started thinking you two were in on Sal Mancini's plan to take him down. Some time back he started doing business with a certain Mexican drug cartel, and it's made him more powerful and more paranoid. He thought that if you turned up dead while on the run he could still convince the Mancinis that he wasn't involved in Sal's murder."

"How did you figure all of this out?"

"I went to meet with Gianni Zanetti."

"How did you arrange that?"

"Let's just say he was incentivized. I knew he had someone working within the FBI, but I didn't know who—not until I saw him take a call from his man inside immediately following the gunfight in St. Thomas. It didn't take much to learn that Conrad and Richter were the only agents on the scene, and I knew it wasn't Conrad."

"Your dad helped us nail Richter," said McGuinness. "Once we knew where to look, all it took was a couple of bugs and some phone records."

"By the time Richter told me you were in Aruba," Declan continued, "you had already set sail. I was afraid you'd be heading north into the storm, so McGuinness put the Coast Guard on alert. They weren't far off when I got Misty's call. You got lucky. It's a good thing this girl has more sense than you."

Grey lay back down and closed his eyes, absorbing the complexity of the bizarre and almost unbelievable story.

"So, Zanetti and Richter," he said, "you got them?"

"They're locked up," said Agent Sanborn. "Richter will never again see the light of day, and we have a solid case against Zanetti too. Conrad is coming back to Chicago with me to help us see that he gets justice."

"I heard about some shootings in Chicago. Some sniper. Did that have anything to do with us?"

"There is no sniper," McGuinness interjected. "He doesn't exist. I hate to cut this short, but Carla and I have a flight to catch. Grey," he said, extending his hand, "I'm glad this didn't end worse. Thanks for staying alive."

"You're welcome, Agent McGuinness," Grey replied, shaking his hand. "There's nothing more satisfying than making a friend of a foe."

Declan stood to walk them out, but Grey stopped him.

"Dad," he said, "I'm sorry about your friend, Tobias."

"That ornery son of a bitch is right down the hall," Declan laughed. "He was angrier about me pulling him back to the States than he was about being shot."

They stepped out of the room leaving Grey and Misty alone. She pulled her chair closer and rested her head on his chest. He ran his fingers through her hair and down the soft skin of her cheek.

"I heard the Star Silo has a new investor," she said. "They're going to finish it."

"Really?"

"Yeah. You should be out of here within the week. We can take a ride over to the site when we get home."

"Misty."

"Yes?"

"Are my clothes in the closet there?"

"Yes."

"Will you go check my pants pocket?"

She went to the small corner closet and opened it. "What am I looking for?" she asked, unfolding his clothes.

"The same thing I was looking for before we went overboard. I picked something up for you in St. Thomas."

She reached into the pocket and pulled out a small jewelry box. She cupped it in her hands and looked up at him.

"Grey—"

"Just hang onto that until we get home. Keep it safe. It's traveled a long way."

She looked at the box again for a moment and then slipped it into her pocket and crawled into the single bed beside him, wrapping her arms around him.

"I love you," she said.

"I love you more."

"I'm sorry about the *Mistical Reflection*. I know how much you loved that boat."

"I did," he replied, "but we can build another one."

"How do you think Ankur will feel about having to start over?"

"Somehow I don't think he'll mind."

# Nautical Terminology

**Bow:** the front end of a vessel

**Stern:** the rear end of a vessel

**Fore:** at, near, or toward the bow

**Aft:** at, near, or toward the stern

**Starboard:** the side of a vessel that is on the right when one is facing forward

**Port:** the side of a vessel that is on the left when one is facing forward

**Windward:** into the wind; upwind

**Leeward:** with the wind; downwind

**Beam:** a vessel's breadth at its widest point perpendicular to the centerline

**Sloop:** a sailboat with a single mast and fore-and-aft rig, i.e. sails are set along the centerline of the vessel

**Deck:** the platform over the hull of a vessel serving as the main surface floor and the roof of the cabin below

**Hull:** the main frame and form of a vessel including the sides and bottom

**Keel:** the finlike structure along the centerline at the bottom of a vessel's hull that serves functionally for ballast and lift

**Mast:** the vertical post on a vessel to which the sails are affixed

**Boom:** a spar or pole that runs along the bottom edge of a sail on a fore-and-aft rigged sailboat

**Gunwale:** the top edge along the sides of the hull where it meets the deck

**Brightwork:** the metal hardware and features as well as varnished woodworking

**Porthole:** an exterior window on a vessel, commonly circular in shape

**Cabin:** the living compartment on a vessel

**Berth:** a bed or bedroom on a vessel; also, the place where a vessel rests at anchor or at a wharf

**Head:** the bathroom or toilet on a vessel

**Galley:** the kitchen on a vessel

**Bulkhead:** a wall within a vessel's cabin

**Mainsail:** a vessel's primary sail; on a Bermuda rig, this is a large triangular sail set aft of the mast

**Headsail:** a sail set forward of the mast

**Jib:** the most common type of headsail, triangular in shape

**Genoa:** a large jib that overlaps the mainsail

**Spinnaker:** a large headsail designed for sailing on a reaching or running course

**Mainsheet:** the line, rope, or cable used to control the mainsail

**Jib Sheet:** the line, rope, or cable used to control the headsail

**Tack:** When sailing generally to windward (a sailboat cannot sail directly into the wind), tacking, or coming about, is a maneuver to change course by turning the bow through the wind. A sailboat is also said to be on a starboard or port tack depending on which side of the bow the wind is coming from.

**Close-Hauled:** the point of sail that is as close to windward as possible to still efficiently sail

**Reach:** a point of sail where the wind is coming from the side of the boat

**Beam Reach:** the wind is coming across the beam, i.e. at a right angle to the boat

**Broad Reach:** the wind is coming from a rear angle; between a beam reach and a run

**Run:** the point of sail where the wind is coming directly behind the boat; also called "running before the wind"

**Jibe (Gybe):** When reaching or running, jibing is a maneuver to change course by turning the stern through the wind. Since the sails remain full throughout the maneuver, jibing is generally more dangerous than tacking, particularly when it occurs accidentally as a result of a change in wind direction or a mistake at the helm.

Curtis Krusie, author of *The World as We Know It*, is a practicing commercial real estate professional with a passion for architecture and adventure. He earned his BS at the University of Missouri in human environmental sciences with an emphasis in personal financial planning and a minor in architectural studies and environmental design. He later earned a certificate of specialization in computer-aided drafting and design, during which coursework he met his wife, Bryn, an interior designer and art consultant. Both are marathon runners and advocates for holistic health who enjoy traveling the world together, documenting their journeys via photography and the written word.

Krusie's latest novel, *Reflections in the Mist*, is inspired by his travels through the Caribbean and his lifelong love of architecture.

Made in the USA
Columbia, SC
09 September 2017